SubWay Dancer

and Other Stories

Catherine Ryan Hyde

Edition: April 2013

SUBWAY DANCER AND OTHER STORIES is a new collection of gripping short fiction by Catherine Ryan Hyde, the bestselling author of many beloved novels, including DON'T LET ME GO and PAY IT FORWARD, and of other critically acclaimed short story collections, including EARTHQUAKE WEATHER and ALWAYS CHLOE.

A striking and emotionally resonant collection, SUBWAY DANCER AND OTHER STORIES is a compilation of stories originally published in some of the most respected literary magazines in the country, including *The Antioch Review*, *Virginia Quarterly Review*, *Glimmer Train* and *Ploughshares*.

In the award-winning story "Bloodlines," two neighbors of different ethnicities are friends in spite of their differences. . .until an argument about expensive pure-bred dogs versus mutts from the pound brings the whole neighborhood's precarious balance crashing down. "Bloodlines" was reprinted in *Bark Magazine*'s best-selling anthology *Dog is My Co-Pilot* and was cited in *Best American Short Stories*.

In Witness to Breath, a woman living a dangerous life working on the streets takes in an elderly dog left behind when his owner is killed in a robbery. Despite never having been a dog person, their brief relationship changes her in ways she never could have expected.

In Disappearances, a man not fluent in his own emotions tries unsuccessfully to broadside a train in his pickup truck, then spends the rest of the story figuring out the first clue to why he'd try to do such a thing. Among the other riveting and beautifully crafted stories included in this collection, "Five Singing Gardeners and One Dead Stranger" and "Requiem For a Flamer" were nominated for the Pushcart Prize, and "The Man Who Found You in the Woods" was cited in *Best American Short Stories*.

This collection includes an Author's Note by Catherine Ryan Hyde.

Subway Dancer

BLUE DOG IN THE CRAZY TRUCK

I have to tell you this story so I can tell you the real one.

When Pippin and I were both seven, my father and I were taking her for a walk. We were passing in front of that little store on the next block, which had been boarded up for years, only on that day some new business was moving in. Three big guys were wheeling stuff on dollies, stuff like refrigerator cases and big metal shelves. They had their T-shirt sleeves rolled high, all three of them, sweating in the heat. They all looked a little bit alike, wheeling stuff from a moving van at the curb, passing each other on the sidewalk. Just as we crossed in front of their shop, Pippin stopped and squatted down, and I prayed all she would do was pee. Two of the guys just stopped, and a minute later the third came out and he stood and stared at us, too, with his hands on his hips. Staring at this smelly little pile on their pavement.

Well, I should make this a shorter story, since it's not even the really important one.

The guys said, "Clean it up." And my father said,

"Come on. Give me a break. With what? My hands?"
And the guys said, "Clean it up, or we're going to call
the police," and that's when I noticed they were all a
lot bigger than him. That my father wasn't as big as I
always thought he was. "Okay," he said, "no need for
that." They brought him a skimpy little paper napkin
from inside the shop.

When we got home, he told the story to my mother.
Only when he got to the part about them calling the
police, he claimed to have said, "Oh, come on, you're
not going to call the police." Right in front of me
he told it like that. Like I wasn't right there when it
happened.

That's when I learned about shame, which always
feels more painful on someone else's behalf.

Less than a year later my mother divorced us, and
I didn't see much of her after that. I always figured
she must have seen it, too, somehow. Seen some little
glimpse of what I'd seen. So now we both knew he
wasn't quite as big as we thought. And I was his son,
so I must have been what he was, and not been what
he was not, which I think is why she divorced me, too.
That was always my theory, anyway. You need to be
able to explain a thing like that in your head, or you'll
never get to sleep at night. Even an explanation that
basically means you suck is better than no explanation
at all.

Okay. I had to tell you that story so I could tell you
this one.

Pippin and I were thirteen and a half. We didn't live
in western New York near that little store anymore. We

lived in Echo Park in Los Angeles with Alvie. My father and I were taking Pippin for a walk down Alvarado Street. It was late in the evening, maybe eight-thirty, but still—I swear—eighty-five degrees. September, that weird kind of L.A. Indian summer where the smog and the buildings trap the heat and you can't see the sky but you know it's hot, wherever it is.

It's hard for me to say what happened first, how it started, because I was looking at Pippin. She was rooting around at the edge of a vacant lot, looking for a place to pee. Pippin was a Welsh corgi, with legs about four inches long, so when you looked at her, you were looking at the ground, and you didn't see much else, because nothing much goes on at that level.

When I looked up I saw the man. He had greasy dark blond hair, and a tattoo on his jaw. A long vertical cross with a snake crawling along it. Right on his face. Where someone else would have a sideburn, he had this. It was dark where we stood, nowhere near a streetlight, but just for a minute somebody's car lights lit us up. I expected the man's knife to look shiny. I thought that was part of the dangerousness of the knife. How light was supposed to glint off it into my eyes. But it looked rusty, or just filthy, maybe. Or both. I wanted the person who owned the car lights to stop and help. Things were being said. I guess they must have been. I could hear them, in a way. I remember the sound of voices, but not what was said. My father took off his watch and handed it over.

I got that feeling again. That same feeling like watching him pick up dog shit with this tiny little skimpy napkin that barely covered his hand, with all those big guys watching. I know it's not fair that I felt that. Believe me, I know. I'm just telling you what I felt. I'm not saying it's fair.

At a moment like that you think things, and you feel things, and they happen fast. They don't ask permission. They're not always even important thoughts, and they don't always make good sense.

Like, I thought, Jesus Christ, guy, at least take care of your knife. I mean, you're a robber, a mugger, whatever. This is a tool of your trade.

And I thought it was good he was a white guy like me and my father, because it would be really hard to go home and tell Alvie a black guy mugged my father and sliced him up with a rusty blade and left him bleeding onto Alvarado Street. It would've hurt me to tell Alvie that, because it would've hurt her to hear it, in one of those funny little places where things get in and you can't get in after them to take away the sting.

I make it sound like I had lots of time to think about things, but really it all happened fast.

When my father took his watch off to hand it over, he dropped Pippin's leash. And Pippin took off running. And I ran after her. I wondered later if I ran after her because I was afraid for her, which I'm sure was part of it, or if running after something—to something—made it a less obvious example of running away. While I was chasing her I wondered if she was scared. If she was running away, too. But I knew probably not. Pippin would always run if you dropped the leash, as long as I'd known her, which was always. I didn't figure she knew enough about this to run scared. Pippin was always scared of the wrong things. Always trying to defend us from things that didn't matter—like the crazy dog in the blue truck, which I'll tell you about later—and then going off on a romp while some guy sliced up my father. I'd been trying to teach her but she just didn't get it because she was only a dog.

She ran across the street and almost got hit by a car. But the guy squealed on his brakes and stopped in time, and I ran after her, ran by in front of him, with one hand up, like waving. Like, thanks for not killing her, because I've never lived a day she wasn't around. Then a car going the other way actually hit me. Not all that hard, but it did. The guy tried to stop, and maybe another six inches he would have. But the headlight hit my right hip and knocked me down. I didn't even break his headlight, though, and it didn't break me, because I got up and kept running.

Pippin started to wear down after awhile, and I caught her leash and we ran home together. I never once looked over my shoulder. After a while I had to pick her up, because she couldn't run that fast anymore. Being thirteen and those little short legs. Still, she weighed over twenty pounds, and I was running straight uphill. Seven blocks straight uphill from Alvarado Street, that's where we lived with Alvie. I could feel sweat running on my face; my face felt hot, radiating hot, like my skin was letting off heat. My chest burned, but I think I could have run to the top of that hill if I had to, because I had to. Because I had to get home to Alvie. If I could just get home and tell Alvie, somehow this night could be over.

We lived in a court apartment, one of the ones all the way at the top, up the steep stairs. I put Pippin down on her short legs again. Grabbed the handrail, which was a long welded pipe right up the center of the stairs. And all the way up I screamed for her. Alvie. Alvie. Alvie.

When I got to our door she threw it open, and we stood face to face. Just stood like that under the porch light, two mirror faces, and in hers I could see what she saw in mine. She had fine, dark black skin, Alvie. Shiny black, and hair in a river of tiny, neat, perfect braids. Each braid had beads at the end, and I loved the sound they made, the clattering, like a wind chime. It always made Alvie sound more alive than everybody else. But as we stood looking at each other, her hair was perfectly silent. I could see the whites all the way around the chestnut of her eyes.

I waited in Alvie's car while she made the call. Alvie had a big old-fashioned boat of a car, an old Chevy with no hubcaps, but it ran fine. She took good care of the parts that counted, and it always ran. When she got in, I didn't even look over at the side of her face. I didn't want her to look at mine. I was afraid of what she'd see. Afraid she'd look at me and feel shame, like she was watching me clean up dog crap while a bunch of big guys watched.

I didn't use my voice to show her where to drive, I just pointed.

When we got to the corner there was nothing there. Nobody. Like nothing had ever happened. Just a black puddle, like somebody drove their car up on the sidewalk and then spilled their dirty crankcase oil. Alvie always carried a flashlight under her seat. She had a knack for practical things like that, very organized, which is one reason my father and I needed her so much.

We got out and stood on the corner together, and Alvie shined her flashlight on that puddle, and it turned red. The black had only been a trick of the light.

Alvie spoke three words under her breath. But I don't know what they were. Maybe because of that sweet, thick accent, or just the way she hushed them. Maybe she wasn't even speaking English just then. I think they had something to do with praying to God but that's only a gut impression. Really I had no way to know.

At the hospital I told everyone Alvie was my stepmother. It should have been the other way around. She was practically his wife, and she should have been telling them I was his son, and defending my right to be there. But she wasn't his wife, not really, and they were more interested in blood. Blood relations. Which made Alvie a poor relation, standing behind me while I tried to explain.

I told one nurse Alvie was my mother, just to see the look on the nurse's face. Just to see her do what I knew she would, look from Alvie's exotic blackness to my own towhead and freckles and back again. I wanted to say, "Fuck you," to her, but I knew I'd regret it later, because it wasn't her fault my father got cut.

"The boy exaggerates," Alvie said, drawing it out song-like and thick, her accent still more proof that I was a liar.

The nurse shook her head as if she could shake us away for the night.

While we sat in the waiting room, while my father lay on that operating table, I confessed a sin to Alvie. It was the first either of us had spoken in nearly an hour, and it startled us both to hear the sound of my voice.

"Alvie," I said. "I told my friends from school that you were from Jamaica."

What this had to do with the moment I could not have explained. But now I see it was something about that nurse. How she took something away from Alvie—something that rightly belonged to her—by knowing at a glance we were not blood relatives. And then, sitting waiting for my father to make it through surgery or die on the table, it dawned on me that I had stolen from Alvie, too. I had stolen her heritage for selfish gains. For stupid reasons, like the word Haiti sounding like the word hate. And Jamaica being a place you go for a vacation, to lie on white sand and drink rum. And Haiti being a place where Papa Doc and Baby strung innocent people from trees and wouldn't allow their neighbors to cut them down and put their bodies to rest in the ground.

"Why would you say that, Neal? You know where I'm from."

"Yes," I said. "I know. I'm sorry."

She looked at me for a moment. It seemed like a long moment. I prayed I wouldn't look too small to her. Then she set her mouth strangely and shook her head. I knew she would ask no more about it. It had flown away from her mind.

"Why didn't you do something, Neal?"

My stomach chilled strangely, and for the first time I realized my hip hurt. It wasn't injured exactly, but it was pretty bruised up, and the sensation broke through, for the first time, and I noticed that.

"Like what?" I said.

"Scream, or run out and stop traffic."

"I don't know."

My eyes were squeezed shut, so it startled me when she grabbed me. We were sitting on a vinyl couch together, and she threw her arms around me, and pulled me in against her, and pulled my head to her shoulder. Then my eyes opened, and stayed that way, like they might never close again. I could see the clock on the waiting room wall, and hear Alvie's hair clattering loud against my ear.

"Oh, Nealy," she said. "Please forget I said that. Please?"

I nodded. But of course I would not forget it. How could I? What a gift for words, to be able to take all that free-floating guilt, all those questions, all that hindsight, and force it to the ground in five simple words. The five words I'd been searching for myself. And Alvie found them for me. Why didn't I do something?

"It wasn't your fault, Nealy. It wasn't." Nobody had called me Nealy for years. At any other time I might have objected. Then she found five more words, and I wouldn't forget these, either. "You're only a little boy. You couldn't have done anything, Nealy. You're only a little boy."

Alvie stood behind me, one hand on each of my shoulders, while I talked to the police. I was good, too. For the first time all night, I did something right. They loved the part about the tattoo, because once you know that, who cares if he was five-ten or six feet and who cares what he was wearing because he can change his clothes, anyway. I liked it too because I knew I wouldn't have to go in to look at a lineup unless they really got him, because if it wasn't him they'd know, without my help. I even told them things I didn't know I'd seen until I told them. The way the guy smiled like a dog showing his teeth, and how when the car's lights lit us up I saw a chip broken off his front tooth. I hadn't even known I'd seen that until later. I felt Alvie squeeze my shoulders and I knew she was proud of me.

"Can you officers give the boy a ride home?" she asked.

I'd been telling her, before the cops showed up, that Pippin had never done her business on that walk and somebody should be home with her now. I know Alvie would have cleaned it up. But the hospital was bright and loud and I wanted to go home and sit with Pippin and be nearly alone.

The cops asked if she thought I'd be okay home by myself. She said she'd be home before the night was over, and after all I was not a child, I was nearly fourteen years old. You see, I'd grown older in just those few minutes, and Alvie knew it and vouched for it. I liked that about Alvie. She wasn't afraid to allow for change.

Just before we all three left together, the two cops and me, Alvie pulled me around by my elbow and whispered in my ear. "Don't let them come in," she said, and I remembered that Alvie and my father had been smoking Alvie's bong just before we went out for that walk.

When I got inside by myself, the apartment was dark. Just the glow of the corner streetlight shining through the contact-papered windows, patterned to look like stained glass. Alvie liked them that way because she could leave the bong and the bag out on the table and no one could see in. Alvie's orange-and-white cat was sitting on the back of the couch, looking like a saint in that stained glass glow. The way he looked at me felt like a blessing. I hid everything illegal in my father's dresser drawer, for no real reason I could pin down.

I took a shower because I stank, because all that dried sweat felt uncomfortable, because it was all part of the man with the cross and the snake and the chipped tooth. All his fault, all his doing. I stood in the hot water until it turned cold, and then I put on just pajama bottoms. Eased them over my bruised hip, and then pulled them down again to look at the bruise in the mirror.

I took Pippin out to the very closest patch of dirt, and the whole time she was circling around I kept looking behind me.

Then I sat on the window seat in my room, and Pippin sat up there with me, but I had to lift her up there because her legs were too short. My window was the only one with no contact paper. I liked to see out.

Pippin growled low in her throat and then a minute

later I heard him. Pippin always heard him first. The barking, and the low pop of that truck engine. The blue truck was a big, old thing with rust primer spots, and a beefy engine, and not much muffler. It came by every night in the middle of the night, then back up the hill in the early, still-dark morning. The downhill run made the valves pop, a little explosion like a backfire on every cylinder, and I think that dog was crazy, because he barked the whole time. Everywhere that truck went, he ran back and forth in the bed and barked. Pippin hated him. Pippin wanted to save me from him. That's why I started calling him "just the crazy dog in the blue truck." It made him sound less important. I was trying to teach Pippin what was important.

But that night my voice sounded like somebody else's, small and far away. Tinny. Unfamiliar. "It's okay, Pippin," I said, "it's just the blue dog in the crazy truck." It wasn't until I heard myself say it that I noticed I'd screwed it up, and then it didn't seem to matter.

When Alvie came in the front door I didn't get up. I just waited for her to find me.

She came into my room and stood near the window seat. She put one of her hands on my bare shoulder. Alvie's long fingernails were gone. Those gorgeous, perfectly manicured nails with the peach-colored polish; she'd bitten them off. I was so used to her fingers ending that beautiful way. It was a shock to me, like seeing her with the ends of her fingers cut off, or with her eyelashes and eyebrows shaved, or with no teeth. Things that had always been there, missing.

"He's out of surgery," she said.

"How do they think it looks?"

"Touch and go, Nealy. Touch and go. The doctor is worried about infection. Because his intestine was cut."

"Peritonitis," I said. I had a friend at summer camp who almost died of peritonitis when his appendix burst. Almost died. But he didn't die. He lived to tell me the story.

"Come on, Nealy," she said. "You need to get some sleep."

She took me by the hand and led me over to my bed, and I lay down on top of the covers. It was still too hot to cover up. Then she left the room for a while, and I could hear her moving around the house, but I have no idea what all she did.

A few minutes later she came back into my room and lay down on the bed behind me. Not exactly touching me, but close enough that I knew by feel how close she was. I felt her fingers on my scalp, front to back, stroking my hair the way you might stroke a worry stone. Over and over. Immediately I got an erection, and I lay there thinking about my father lying in the hospital, but that didn't make it go away. I thought, Jesus Christ, Neal, what kind of monster are you? But I couldn't do a damn thing about it, except to stay faced away and not make a statement on whether I was awake or not. She kept that rhythm in my hair, but never really touched me beyond that, except that she set her head right behind mine on the pillow, and part of her face rested on my neck. When she breathed through that fine, wide nose, I could feel the light brush of her breath across my collarbone, like a cool touch. I don't know how long we stayed like that but it must have been near morning, because Blue Dog came back up the hill. I heard Pippin growl in her throat. That's the first I let on I was awake.

"It's okay, Pippin," I said. "It's only the blue dog in the crazy truck."

"What on earth are you talking about?" Alvie said, with no real reproach or judgment.

"Nothing. It's just a private joke with me and Pippin. I'm trying to teach her what's dangerous and what's not."

"She's only a dog, Nealy."

"I know that."

"She's an old dog. If she doesn't know by now, I think she won't learn."

"I know," I said. "It's just a game."

The side window in my room was open for the breeze, and I lay still and thought about the man with the book and the razor. He'd visited five women in Echo Park the previous summer, and the police never caught him. He came in hot weather, cut their screens with a razor blade. Stood over their beds and exposed himself, with a book in front of his face so they could never identify him.

Now that's dangerous, Pippin.

And I was home alone with Alvie. What would I do if something bad happened to Alvie and my father wasn't around? How much good would I be?

I lay there, still hard, thinking about that man, wondering if I was any better than him, any safer to be around. I tried to send silent signals to Pippin to be extra watchful, but then I could hear her snoring in the corner. I decided I'd have to stay awake to keep everybody safe.

Alvie woke me with a kiss on the temple. She was standing over my bed, fully dressed. Her hair clattered as she straightened up again. I usually woke up with a hard-on anyway, so I went to pull the covers up, but they were up already. Alvie must have covered me in my sleep.

She was wearing jeans and her "I am your witness" T-shirt—the one she bought at a fund-raiser for all the women victims of the rape camps in Bosnia—and one of my father's denim shirts open over it, like a jacket, so you couldn't read all of what it said. But I knew it by heart, except the parts that weren't in English.

"Are you going to school?" she asked.

"No."

"Okay. You can come to the hospital, but you'll have to move very fast."

But I couldn't get up right then in front of her, so I said, "You go on, Alvie. I'll take the bus down in a little while." I knew she wanted to leave right then, anyway.

"Do you have bus fare?"

"Yes."

She wasn't thinking clearly. I had a bus pass to go to school. It cost no more to go to the hospital. She kissed me again, this time on the forehead, and swept out of the room. And I wondered if she'd sleep in my bed again that night.

Then it hit me, really hit me for maybe the first time, that he might die. And then Alvie would sleep in my bed every night. We'd have to be very quiet about it at first, but after a few years I'd be eighteen, and we could move somewhere nobody knew us, and if they had a problem with the difference in our ages or our colors, they could go fuck themselves. It was none of their concern. But then my father would have died. I lay there with my perpetual erection thinking, Jesus Christ, Neal. What kind of monster are you?

But he wasn't going to die, anyway. He was going to pull through. And Alvie was going to go back to sleeping in bed with him like she always had. Like last night had never happened.

It was like the lady or the tiger except in that story one of the guy's possibilities is good.

That night I came home from the hospital in a cab, and I waited three hours for Alvie to join me. I showered, and wore only pajama bottoms like the night before, and covered myself with a sheet in spite of the heat, all because I expected her.

If I'm remembering correctly, I was hard before she ever arrived. And I don't know what kind of monster I was. I don't know. Things just are sometimes.

When she got home she changed into one of my father's long shirts, and lifted up the sheet and got underneath with me. Instead of stroking her fingers through my hair she placed one smooth, light-caramel palm across my forehead, like she was checking me for fever, and just held it there, unchanging. She kissed the back of my hair lightly.

"What did they say, Alvie?"

"Same thing they were saying before you left."

"Still not awake."

"No. Doctor says the next twenty-four hours will tell."

"He said that before I left."

"What did I just tell you?"

What I'd meant was, shouldn't it be twenty-one hours by now? It seemed wrong to keep pointing to twenty-four hours that never got shorter, like waiting for a school bell that's always three hours away.

We lay quietly for a long time, and she was close enough I could feel her breasts through my father's shirt, feel them up against my back.

"I called your grandparents," she said. "They'd be very happy to have you. If . . . You know. If. If it should come to that. But they also said you're a big boy, you can decide for yourself who you want to live with."

"I want to stay with you, Alvie."

"Hush!" She barked the word at my ear, tugged at my forehead in a sharp gesture that felt almost like a slap. I stopped breathing briefly. "It's not time to claim such things. You don't make that choice yet. Because maybe there will be no choice to make."

"Right. You're right, Alvie. Probably not."

We both breathed again, and I felt her thumb move on my forehead, stroking me just the tiniest bit. "I would take care of you, though." She breathed it against my ear, so small, like if she said it quietly enough, God couldn't hear it and act on it.

I knew then that what I thought I'd felt the night

23

before I really had felt, even though nothing had happened on the outside. Someone could have been there watching and never seen it, but I knew then it was real. I wanted to say, We'd take care of each other, Alvie, but I didn't want her to bark at me again.

Speaking of barking, a few minutes later he came down the hill, valves popping, and Pippin growled at him.

"Blue dog in the crazy truck," Alvie said.

"Blue dog," I said, feeling we had the beginnings of a language now. Knowing if my father were here, he wouldn't know what we meant.

Just before I fell sleep she said, "Neal."

And I said, "What, Alvie?"

"Do you know what he would have said to do, if there had been time? If he hadn't had the knife to watch, if it hadn't all happened so fast? Do you know what he would have told you?"

"No, Alvie. What?"

"He would have said, 'Run, Nealy. Run away.' And when you got away safe he would have been so happy."

I closed my eyes again and later I had a dream, and in the dream I was running away, and I could hear my father yelling to me, and sure enough, that's what he was saying. "Run, Nealy. Get away." So I was only doing what he wanted me to do, and I was making him happy. Only in the dream Pippin got hit by a car. So, once something like that happens in your life, almost no matter how it turns out, it seems like something will be lost.

The phone woke us. Alvie reached over me to pick up my extension, her body pressing against my back, pushing me forward.

"Yes, this is she," she said. And then, "Thank you so much. I'll be right down."

She hung up the phone and got out of bed, taking the crush of her body away.

"He woke up," she said. "They've upgraded him to stable."

I sat up and blinked. Watched her walk out of my room without saying more, without looking back, without saying goodbye. Something had blown out of her when this new information blew in, like there was only just so much room inside her to feel.

In the same way I understood the realness of what we'd felt, I just as clearly understood that what we'd felt was now over.

My father came home three days later. I wasn't there when he arrived; I was out walking Pippin. We'd been walking two, three, sometimes four miles a day, because I knew if I let myself I could lose the habit of ever walking down a street again. It was like overkill.

And, actually, it was not a surprise to me. I'd gone out walking that day knowing damn well she'd gone to the hospital to bring him home.

I walked into their bedroom. He was lying on his back in bed, with a sheet pulled up to his armpits. Alvie was lying beside him, stroking her fingers through his hair. Just for a minute that stopped me, literally. I just stopped in my tracks and looked at both of them, and none of us said a word. With his eyes my father said, You come over here and sit down with me, and with her eyes Alvie said, It was between us; you never say a word about it.

And I never did.

I sat down beside my father and he grabbed my hand too hard. I expected him to say something coherent and meaningful but he was still doped up on painkillers. I expected him to look small like he'd been doing lately, but instead he just looked so damn much bigger than me.

I let him squeeze my hand too hard. I purposely didn't look at Alvie because if I had I couldn't have said what I said next, even though I didn't say it out loud.

But what I said to him, in the privacy of my own gut, was this: She's the most important thing I ever had in my life, but I'm giving her back to you, because I'm that happy you're alive.

Of course I knew in my head she wasn't mine to keep or give back, but I told you already, this was my gut.

Also, guts don't give up neatly, so after that not a day went by I didn't regret the gift, wrestle with it, resent it, long to change my mind. But just at that moment I said it to him, silently, and believed I meant it, and that felt like enough.

BLOODLINES

Me and my neighbor Frank Main used to get along real good till the dog thing. We got two kids each, only a year apart in school, and his wife and my wife take turns sometimes driving carpool. I took his mail in every day for two weeks while they had their vacation, and once when I dropped an intake manifold on my foot, Frank mowed my lawn for five weeks running. I think he's one of those America-America guys, like, you're here now, so speak English, but in nine years he never once made fun of my English—even at the beginning when it wasn't so good—or mentioned nothing about it. Like so long as I was trying, you know? I got mixed feelings about that but it never much got in our way.

Anyhow, a while back his boy, Eddie, got after him to get a dog. And I even put in my two cents. I said you'll never regret it, Frank, it's the best move ever. I said look what Blackie is to our family. The kids love her, she takes care of the house, she even gets me off my lazy behind to walk her every morning and every night and that's good for the both of us.

She's the best dog, Blackie, big as a house, nearly

eighty pounds, I think, though I never picked her up and put her on a scale, but so gentle. Shepherd and some Labrador and maybe something else, too. She can see her favorite food in my son's hand, a big juicy piece of steak, maybe, and she'll take it so gentle he'll giggle because he says it tickles his hand. And to think a dog like that was on her last day at the pound. Just think, Frank, I said, you could save a life like that, too, and that dog'll pay you back in more ways than you even knew there were.

So I felt real good the day he leaned over the fence and said he found the perfect dog.

Great, I said, when are you bringing him home? I can't wait to see. Is it a male dog or female?

Not sure, he said. Haven't decided yet. The bitch is expected to whelp in three weeks, then the breeder likes to let 'em nurse seven or eight weeks before he weans 'em—that makes 'em nice and confident since they're born guard dogs—and then me and Eddie get our pick of the litter and we'll be bringing it on home.

Now wait, I said, now hold on a minute here, let me get something straight. You found the perfect dog but it isn't even born yet? He just smiled in a way that made me see the first of the trouble coming on. Then how do you know it's perfect? You got a crystal ball to look in?

Researched it, he said. Bloodlines. Pedigree papers. Red Doberman pinscher, championship lines. Be a hell of a watchdog.

By now I could already feel things get hot behind my ears. This is never a good sign.

Blackie is a hell of a watchdog, I said. And she was

nearly free, out of the county pound. One time Blackie just out of nowhere howled like a banshee and lit out across the yard and leaped up at a spot on the corner of the fence. Slammed right into the fence and brought us running. We had no idea why but in a few minutes later some creep was caught looking over the back fence at widow Jesperson's place down the street.

Like I said, Blackie is big as a house, and if she were to say to you, Stay out of my family's yard, I just bet you would. I just damn well bet you would.

I didn't think I should ask how much this pure red Doberman was costing him, but I wanted to know real bad.

Anyhow, I could see things going in a wrong direction, so I just took a few big deep breaths and I said to myself, It's a free country, man can get any dog he wants. Man can do what he wants, even if it's stupid. So all I said was, Can't wait to see, Frank, and then I went inside to take it out on my poor wife.

If I made the America laws, I said to my poor wife, who was trying to finish the lunch dishes, a guy could still do what Frank is doing, only first he'd have to go to the pound and walk up and down all those rows and look in the eyes of all those smart, pretty dogs, and tell them why they're just not good enough. Why they gotta die while he's waiting for something better to get born. And another thing, I said. What kind of example is that to set for your kids? Here's how much we respect life, kids. Let's make sure lots of new dogs get born even though we're killing half the ones that are already here. 'Cause, you know, our dog has to be special. And another thing. I wonder what he's paying for that dog. What do you think, Sofi? Guess.

I couldn't guess, Cacho, she said. I got no idea. Probably a lot.

Just my point. Just what I'm saying. Probably a lot.

Then she dried her hands and touched my shoulder like she does when she wants me to breathe deep and think on happier things. And I swear I thought no more about it till that dog come home.

Now there are crimes against nature and there are crimes against nature, but please tell me why, if the good Lord put a certain set of parts on a dog, why would a guy go and cut some of them off again? Would you tell me that, please? Does Frank Main know more about dogs than God does? Is that it? I'm not trying to be a smartass. I really want to know.

I seen lots of dogs with tails cut off but it's still a crime against nature if you ask me. But then Frank tells me he's going to have the vet cut off half of those pretty silky ears and tape what's left to splints so they'll stick up straight.

While he's telling me this the pup is sitting on one hip, all off at an angle, and she turns her head to follow some movement, a bird or a fly, I don't know, and almost falls right over. For all that money I don't think she's very smart. But that doesn't make it right what he's saying. She's flesh and blood, after all.

Why? I ask him. That's all I want to know. Why take a knife to a healthy pup?

She's purebred Dobie, he says. Got to at least look like one.

Then he goes inside before we can really talk any more about it, and the pup—Gretta, he calls her—starts chewing on one of his wife's marigolds in the nice planted beds. I stand and watch over the fence, and she gets tired of the flower after a time and digs up the whole plant. Frank's wife, Sharon, loves those flowers. Doesn't he know you can't just leave a new pup alone like that? They need tending. Figures Frank doesn't know nothing about dogs or he wouldn't be cutting parts off them. Anyhow, puppies are always trouble. Gotta watch them every minute. Blackie was fourteen months when we got her. It's better that way, because all those bad stages are over and besides, people don't like to take the grown ones. They die a lot more regular in the pound. It's stupid, too, because they're better dogs and they get to love you just fine and if you can't train them it just means you don't know nothing about dogs. They're better dogs but they die a lot more regular.

Frank's pup looks up at me with eyes that don't look so smart for all that money.

Blackie never digs up the yard. Blackie is a great dog.

Over the next month or two I get real good at how not to look over the fence. She may be raising hell over there, chewing up landscape and digging for China, but I'll say one thing for that dog, she never makes a sound. Never hear a bark out of her. Sometimes I used to hear Eddie come out and play with her, yell at her to fetch and stuff but it seems like he never does no more.

Like he's back playing with his friends and forgot all about her. The girl is a year younger. She used to go out on the weekend but I guess that dog is too rough for her, because she always ran inside crying. This is all I can hear and I've taught myself not to look over the fence.

I think it's funny how this championship watchdog never barks.

One day I'm walking Blackie, a Monday, a couple hours before work, and here comes Frank and Gretta. She looks nearly half grown now, big enough to pull him down the street. Her ears are taped and she's just crazy. I mean this is one hyper dog. Since this is the first I bumped into them outside the yard, I guess I see why. I'm not saying they never went out before, just I never bumped into them and I'm out two times a day like clockwork. So we walk together for about three blocks, and the pup is scrambling, churning her legs three times for every one of Blackie's steps, like running in place, like overdrive. She's jumping up at Blackie, slamming at her side, and Blackie doesn't hardly notice. Frank is telling me how he hired some pro painter guys to come over and paint his house. I'm looking at the tape all around this poor dog's butchered ears and listening to the paint thing and thinking this just keeps getting stranger.

You should've told me, I say. I'd've pitched in. Two weekends we'd get it done.

No, that's okay, Frank says. Get the pros, they do a good job.

So for a minute I'm thinking, What, I wouldn't do a good job? And I almost say it. But then Frank turns for home. They been out all of six minutes.

What, that's it? I say. Poor dog needs more exercise than that.

I gotta go, he says. Gotta get to the office.

He never said the office before. He always called it work. Just work. He works in a big office on the sixteenth floor downtown and I work in a city garage, maintaining service vehicles. I call it work and he calls it work, but all of a sudden it's the office. Then I think maybe I'm reading too much in.

Let me have her, then, I say. Blackie and me are going all the way down to Figueroa. I'll put her in your yard after.

Sure, I guess, he says. Thanks. Yeah, good. Thanks.

He turns back and I take hold of this little hellion by her stitched leather leash, and man, can that little girl pull. After a while I get tired of hearing her choke herself, so I break from a walk to a jog. It's been a while since I jogged. Months, and even then it wasn't regular. So it hurts my chest but feels kind of good, too, and I go through that wall like I always used to. You know, where you think you can't go more but you do, and then you settle in and get past it and kind of chug along. Blackie loves it. She's loping like a rocking horse, throwing herself up in the air instead of stretching out, so she won't get ahead of me.

I should get back to jogging, I decide. Every day.

A young woman comes out on her stoop to get her morning paper, and while she bends over she sees Gretta and her ear tape and gives me a bad look. One of those "How could you?" looks.

Not my dog, I say.

Either she doesn't believe me or she's mad at me anyhow.

When we get back, Frank is just heading out to his car for work. Oh, excuse me, the office.

You know, it's not just me, I say, and he looks at me funny. I say, Wherever I went with this dog, people think it's not right to put her through that.

Through what? Frank says.

The cropping.

That's what Frank calls it. Cropping. I call it taking a scalpel and slicing up one of God's perfect creatures, but I'm trying to have a civil conversation with the guy.

Oh, that, he says. It's part of what makes 'em good dogs. Makes 'em more stoic, you know?

Actually, I'm not sure I do. I heard the word stoic before, and maybe I knew what it meant at the time, but I can't make it come back to me now.

Frank keeps talking. They get used to pain, and they're better dogs for it.

Stoic. Right. I got it now. All of a sudden I'm mad. Real mad. Last time I got this mad I was still living with my father in Argentina. Now that my father is far away I don't get so mad anymore. Till now. I say something really loud. I say, What? Really loud I yell it and Gretta pees, right there, without even squatting down. It just leaks right out of her. I'm right up in Frank's face and I don't even remember how I got there. My brain knows I'm not going to hit him but my fist can remember how it will feel.

Want me to make you stoic, Frank? I ask him that. I say, You'll be a better man for it.

I just want him to think what he's saying, that's all. How it sounds, what he's saying.

You do it, he says, and I'll have the cops on you so fast.

Then he goes to his car. Leaves me to put his prize dog away in the yard.

We don't talk again for three months. Every morning and every night I take Gretta out of his yard and she jogs with us, but we never talk, me and Frank.

You never know who somebody is. You think you know but you don't.

Then after three months I come home from our run and I have to talk to Frank, to tell him Gretta's spotting. Tell him I can't take her for runs till she's done being in heat because I can't defend her. Had to practically kick two big males to keep them away. We barely made it home. Poor Gretta. She's gotta feel bad when she loses those runs. It's pretty much all she's got.

So I knock on his door.

I tell him all the stuff the vet told us about Blackie. Tell him it can happen to anybody, that our Blackie got in one surprise heat, too, before we got her spayed. That she has to be locked in the house or she'll get pregnant, and now the vet won't spay her till the heat is over.

From the look on Frank's face you'd think I just

explained the whole thing to him in Spanish.

Spay? he says.

Yeah. Spay. Fix. Neuter.

Spay? he says again. He just can't seem to wrap his head around that word. You think I'm going to get a two-thousand-dollar dog spayed?

Two thousand dollars. Two thousand dollars is more than I ever thought, even when I was guessing high. And I decide I'm not going to say all the stuff I want to say to him because he will never see a thing my way. We'll just keep banging heads. I'll say there's too many puppies in the world and he'll say people want champion Dobies, so these'll get homes. And I'll say that don't matter, it's still homes snatched right out from under those that're already here, and he'll say the people who buy his puppies were never headed for the pound no matter what. And then he'll slam the door in my face. Or worse yet, I'll really hit him this time, and the cops will come, and I'll be the wrong one, and all the shame will be mine.

Better keep her locked up in the house, then, I say.

Sharon doesn't like her in the house. Dog won't housebreak.

All dogs housebreak. I don't say this out loud, but it's true. Any dog'll housebreak. Just lots of people don't know how to go about it.

Might have to build her a five-sided run, then, I say.

I see in Frank's face that he doesn't want my advice, any of it, never did. Two thousand dollars. I bought my last car for less than that and it's a good car. Sofi drives it now and it still runs good.

The yard is nice and secure, he says.

I start up to tell him that he doesn't know what a female in heat will do to get out, what the males will do to get at her. But Frank closes the door. Doesn't slam it, but closes it, and me and Blackie and Gretta are on the street on our own. Doesn't even take his damn two-thousand-dollar dog back. I have to put her away in the yard.

While I do I look at Frank's house, all nice with its new paint, and I realize his house is a little nicer than mine. I never noticed that before it was painted. I knew it was bigger but I didn't think about it as nicer. And even in the month or so since the pro paint job, it's sort of been there to see without me seeing it.

Like a lot of other things I guess.

The next thing that happens is so not avoidable I almost don't have to tell it. It practically tells itself. I'm in the back room that Saturday with the windows open for air, and I hear some commotion, some scuffling and whimpering, so I go out, and I look over the fence. A dog is digging through from the other side. I can see his nose now and then, and his paws flying, and Gretta right at the fence cheering him on. Digging from her side, too. Then he tries to squeeze through, doesn't make it on the first try, has to back out and dig more. But I get a good look. And I run get my Polaroid.

When you work on cars, a Polaroid is a good thing to have. Take pictures of all the smog fittings and stuff or you won't never get them back where they go. Take pictures of parts and then post them for sale. Take pictures of ugly mongrel dogs in your neighbor's yard with his prize bitch.

I get back out and the dog is through the fence and Gretta and him are going at it and let me tell you, he's even uglier than I thought. He's got some wire-haired something in him, but a big head like a basset mixed with an Airedale and a million other things. I'm a big lover of dogs and no stickler for beautiful but this is an eyesore of a dog if there ever was one. You almost got to love him for looking so bad.

They're holding still now and they're in that part I think where they're tied and they couldn't come apart if they tried. People don't know that. They'll turn a hose on two dogs and think they're just too into it to stop, but that male is tied in there till it goes down and he's not going nowhere till it's over. I snap off a couple of shots.

I take them inside and watch them turn into pictures, and they come out pretty good. First I think I just won't tell him. After all, I warned him once already. If I told him, he could go to the vet and get it aborted early. If I don't we all get to see what those damn puppies look like. That brings a smile on my face, I got to admit. But then I think it wouldn't be Frank to get hurt, it would be the puppies. One thing I know for damn sure, two people get into it over a dog, the loser will be the dog.

But I don't want any fistfights, so I tell Sharon. I wait till the next morning, when she's out tending the garden. Trying to put it back to where it was before Gretta, I should say. Sharon is crouching down, sweaty, and Gretta is on a chain.

Good morning, I say.

She jumps. Oh. Hi. Yeah.

Why is Gretta chained? I didn't mean to ask. This will get us off on a bad foot.

Oh. Frank said she tried to dig out under the fence.

She didn't, though. I tell Sharon that. I say, A male dug in and got her pregnant. I just wanted you guys to know that. So you can figure what you want to do.

See? After all that's happened I'm still trying to be a good neighbor to this man. That's who I am. Whatever Frank is, that's what I am. The dirt has been half-assed filled in where it was dug.

Sharon wipes her face off on the back of a gardening glove. Frank says Gretta tried to dig out, she says.

I stand there and say nothing. She doesn't believe me. I can't believe this. She thinks I'm lying? All I have to do is go inside and get those pictures. Polaroids never lie. But I don't. Because, you know why? Because I'm doing too much already, to be a good neighbor. And Frank, he's doing not enough. So, Frank, you got some really ugly mutt puppies in your future and it's nobody's fault but your own.

When Gretta starts to show, Frank calls me at my house. Talks to Sofi. Sofi covers the phone and says Frank wants to know if I actually saw a dog in his yard. If I know anything about who his dog might've bred with.

Tell him to go to hell, I say.

She doesn't. She tells him I don't remember.

Now, I make it sound like we are the only two people

in the neighborhood, me and Frank, but of course not. There's lots of others, they just don't figure in about the dog. Till after she gets pregnant. Then Frank is all over asking people if they saw whose dog it was. Acting as if I saw but won't talk. Acting as if he could've got to the situation in time if I'd talked. How'd it take him so long to figure out the dog was pregnant anyways? I mean, doesn't he ever go out there and look at her?

Anyhow, my neighbors on the other side are the Li family. I don't talk much with them, mainly because they won't talk to me or much of anybody else. Sometimes I try to talk to them about neighborhood things, good things that will help, but they don't want trouble. They don't say it like that but I can see. They say things like Thank you and Yes, yes, over and over and hurry back in the house. But they got a son, Richie, I known him since he was in high school, since they first come here from China, and now he's in graduate school but home for the summer. He wants trouble, if it's the right kind. If it's his kind of trouble.

Richie knocks on our door one night after dinner.

I send the kids upstairs to do homework and I sit with Richie in the family room and Sofi worries around getting us brandy while he tells me Frank came to see him.

Richie says, Like it's my problem his stupid dog got knocked up. Know how much he paid for that dog? Four thousand dollars.

I heard two.

You heard wrong.

Frank told me. Two.

Then that's all he wants you to know.

But also, I think, sometimes things go too many places around a neighborhood, and while they're traveling they get too big.

Richie looks so grown up now. His hair is parted on one side and slicked over. He grew up handsome. He's going to be a business man. A good one.

I didn't know you don't like Frank, I say, because it's coming out while he talks.

Of course I don't like him, he's a bigot. You don't like him, do you?

Well, I guess I used to, I say. I don't think he's a bigot exactly. Just stupid. Especially about dogs. And maybe a little. . . like he's better than I am.

Richie sits back with his brandy and we both know I just said it. Frank is a bigot. I always knew it, but till I said it out loud to Richie Li, I didn't know. Explain a thing like that.

The purebred dog thing is a riot, Richie says. That dog is so stupid. And a total failure as a watchdog. I hope the ugliest mutt in the world knocked her up.

Probably I shouldn't have done what I did next but it was hard not to.

Wait, I said. Wait till you see.

And I went and got the pictures of the dogs going at it. I guess that's why I took them. Cause that dog was ugly in a way I could never describe. Richie just howled with laughing. I never heard nobody laugh so hard for such a time. And I looked again and it was even funnier with Richie here, because we neither one of us like Frank.

Oh, please can I have one of these? he said.

Don't show Frank, though.

Why not?

And miss the look on his face when he sees those puppies?

But I did give Richie one, and he took it to his father's copy place and made color photocopies, and gave them to all the neighbors that didn't like Frank. You know, people like us and not like Frank. I guess I always knew the block was divided into some like me and some like him but I never felt it deep till this dog thing.

Then every time Frank took this big pregnant dog for a walk, which wasn't very much, the neighbors who were like us got a good laugh behind their hand. I guess it was mean but I didn't do it, anyhow. Richie Li did it. And also Frank deserves it because he's stupid, especially about dogs, and besides he's a bigot.

Now, it seems to me that anytime you do something you probably shouldn't do, you can bet it will come around to bite you.

So a couple evenings before Gretta is due to whelp I get a big knock at my door. The whole family jumps, because it's one of those police knocks. Either that or fire people to say get out right away. One of those shocking trouble knocks.

I answer the door and there stands Frank. He has a paper in his hand, and he holds it up about an inch in front of my face and it's one of the copies Richie Li made of the dog picture. I step out onto the dark front yard and close the door behind me to spare the family from trouble. While I do I'm feeling that cold flutter when you know things are coming to battle. I notice a couple of the neighbors out already. That police knock sure gets attention.

Frank is yelling at me. Yelling that he's trying to sue the people whose dog got into his yard, and here I have evidence and I don't give it to him, I give it to other people in the neighborhood so they can laugh at him. Loud enough so more neighbors come. And it seems funny how they come. Maybe it's just chance but the people behind Frank are people more like Frank. The people behind me I can only guess, because it's getting to be that dog-fighting thing where you don't look away.

None of this seems very much real.

He holds the picture in my face again. You think this is funny? he screams.

God help me, I crack a smile, I can't stop.

It's a little funny, I say. Yes.

Then just as I expect the fight to start for real I hear the voice of Richie Li behind me. Richie says, I think it's fucking hilarious.

That slows things down because Frank can't swing on two men at once.

Richie says, Frank, you know what? No wonder you got no sense of humor about that picture. Because you're a mongrel yourself and you know it.

Frank's face twists around and I notice that I can see the veins under his forehead. Even just with the streetlight I can see. His face is red and there are veins in his temples and it's because his skin is so white.

Excuse me? he says to Richie.

Just what I said, Frank. My family has been nothing

but Chinese for eons. My friend here is from pure Argentine stock. But the only purebred American is the Indian and you're just a big mix of all those people who came later on a boat.

There are more people behind me than I thought and I know they are people like me because I can hear them saying yeah.

Richie says, Isn't that right, Cacho? and slaps a hand down on my shoulder.

Yes, I say. That's right.

It is right, but it's wrong, too, because if somebody looked at Blackie and said mutt like a bad thing I'd kick his ass. But I'm with Richie. But I feel a little bit like I know what it means to be a gun. Like there's a bigger fight and it's not so much about me but I'm the trigger gets pulled.

Frank throws the picture at my face. It's on a heavy stock like thin cardboard and the corner hits my eye. It's a shock to all of a sudden hurt so this must be the fight.

We weave and circle a little on the lawn with our fists ready, not up exactly but balled up and ready. I don't dare look away but I see Sofi standing on our stoop. See her at the corner of my eye, as she was when I raised fists to my father. Back then I looked over to see her face, asking me to please not. Then I looked back at the face of my father and saw all cold. When I did it, he wouldn't hit me back or call the police, only close his heart to me. Which in most ways he already had. Maybe that's why I was mad enough to hit. Maybe that's why I'm here again now. I didn't give Sofi her wish that day. Instead we gather up and run to this country. But I'm running low on countries where I think I can live.

My fists go straight, turn back to hands. I turn my head to look at my wife. To let her know the moment passed this time on its own.

As I do, Frank's fist slams my cheekbone. A good solid punch, enough to knock me back, slap on my brain. But it doesn't knock me down. I was standing for a fight, one leg well back, feet out. I just snap back and then straight again. I hear a little Oooh from the crowd because he really did it, then a sprinkle of cheer from the people more like me because I'm still on my feet. It does make me seem sort of unbeatable.

I turn my back on Frank and go inside with my wife. I will not hit him back. Just go inside with my wife and put ice on my face. He will be the one that hit. He will always have to live with being the one that hit.

It's hard being the one that hit. I almost feel sorry for Frank.

Three days later a For Sale sign goes up on Frank's lawn. But that's not the strangest thing. I come home from work that day and there's no car in his driveway, no dog in the yard. No curtains, and through the windows you can see no nothing. The house is empty. How did he get out so fast? Maybe packed in private for three days, then a moving company took it all while I worked? I never saw nobody move that fast.

Nobody in the neighborhood knows either, but we talk plenty about it.

Then about a couple months later I see Eddie Main down in front of the home improvement store. He's with a box of puppies to give away.

Hey, Eddie, I say, and he goes quiet like maybe he shouldn't talk to me but I can see that for his own money he'll talk to me fine.

I look at the puppies, and there's just two. They're really not so ugly. No puppy is ugly. Puppies are always cute. They're hairy, with brown goofy eyes.

I ask Eddie how many did there used to be.

Only three, he says. Small first litter. Dad palmed one off on a guy at work. This one maybe I found him somebody. They keep coming by and looking. I bet they like him but maybe they wanted something prettier. But maybe they'll come back.

I ask him where his family has been living.

He says they're in a rented place in the valley, but now they bought a house in Chicago.

Chicago, I say. Wow. Such a long way.

Dad says it'll be better there.

It won't, but I don't tell this to Eddie. It will be the same because Frank will bring himself along.

Good luck with the puppies, I say. What if nobody takes them?

Dad says at the end of the day they have to go to the pound.

Of course. That's what always happens to the puppies, I don't say.

Next day before work I go to the pound. Sure enough there's one of Gretta's puppies, sitting in a cage with a whole ocean of pretty Australian puppies with blue and white coats and blue eyes. With that same goofy look on his face.

I say to the pound lady, I'll take that one.

That one, she says. Really.

Of course she's surprised, but he's my fault. My pighead temper got him born so now he's my job.

But you know, he turns out to be a pretty good dog. Not super smart but smart enough. Not the prettiest dog but the kids love him and he's a great companion to Blackie and a pretty decent watchdog.

I think he gets that from the father side.

HURRICANE LAURA

1. The Storm

When you're outdoors at night in a howling gale-force wind, rain whipping into your face, clamping your ancient Weimaraner between your knees so he won't blow away, you need someone to reach out to you. Literally, and otherwise. You need your loved ones around you, if indeed you have some. This is all the more true if the power is out everywhere, leaving you and your old dog in perfect blackness, hedged only by the circle of flashlight you used to walk here, to her house. Even the moon is experiencing an outage. So you need something, and you need it to stop screwing around and arrive.

What you need is for Laura to be the one to open the door. You knock. And you wait. And Gary opens the door. You don't always get what you need.

You've never met Gary before but you know damn well who he is. And from the way his body blocks the narrow path of doorway, from the look that crosses his face—though it's hard to see by just the glow of your flashlight trained to the doormat—you get the uncomfortable feeling that he knows who you are, too. So you assume he has played this scene before. You knew that, somewhere in your gut. Still it bothers you to meet him and see for a fact that it's true.

There's some kind of glow in the house, perhaps a lantern or a candle, which makes you ache all the more to be inside. This is a light place, and you might be safe here. Laura might make you safe, if only you could get to her. If only her husband would let you by.

"I wouldn't do this if it wasn't an emergency," you say.

"Who are you," he asks. He's still blocking the damn doorway, his pajamas whipped by the wind, rain sailing into his face, newly-wet hair flying, eyes squinted. It occurs to you that he must want badly not to let you in. He's really braving the elements on the off chance he can still prevent it.

"Kate Feinstein," you say. "I'm a friend of Laura's."

You want to look at his face when you say that, to see how the news settles in, but you are distracted by her voice from inside the glow. Apparently Gary is distracted, too.

"Kate?" That's what Laura's voice says.

He turns, allowing the door to open more fully. Allowing more wind and rain to whip into the formerly dry, glowing house. You both look up. Actually, you all three look up. Your dog loves Laura, too.

There she is on the stairs. The ghost. This is not the first you've noticed her resemblance to a ghost. She has been ghostlike in your bed in the dark. It's the hair. She's all hair, Laura, and it's all white. Full and wild and down to her waist or below. Must be premature, you always think, because she couldn't be more than mid-forties. Well, late forties; all right. Well, she could be more; she could be anything. But in the meantime she appears to be only that which she lets you see. In good light she looks less ghostly because of the ruddy skin. The Indian-like skin. Makes her look like an Indian princess now half on her way to crone, but so fully in charge of the process it makes you ache just to look. Now in the glow you can't see that, just other ghost factors. The eerie glow of light, and the wind you have allowed in. The white full-length nightgown, and the way your wind billows it back. That and the hair, billowing back. Like a ghost in a wind tunnel. She wouldn't look like all of this if you hadn't come.

The rain is whipping into her foyer now, and it's all your fault. Your dog is wriggling between your knees because you're holding him too tightly. For his own good, but he doesn't like it. He wants to go in where it's warm, and get dry, and see her again, and so do you.

Laura descends two more stairs. "Kate," she says. Like you are the most important person in the world, which is just what you need to be right now. To somebody. One of her hands extends, ghostlike; you want her to hold you, but Gary is still across the door, soaking wet now, apparently a small price to pay to prevent you getting what you want. "Kate, come in and get dry, love. Come in out of the rain."

Laura has spoken. Gary has no choice but to stand aside.

2. The Introduction

You hadn't been in this town long, and you hadn't been in a small town, really. . . ever. You knew no one here except Donald and Eugene, whose e-mails convinced you this would be a swell place to which to move. You didn't know how it is in a small town, how everybody knows you, and what you're up to. Plus you were blissfully but temporarily unaware of other things. You didn't know that pine trees have short life spans and shallow root systems. That they are known for their tendency to topple when wet and blown. You didn't know how seriously to take the media hype on El Niño, and you had never met Laura. Looking back to that time, you must have known some things, but you can no longer recreate what things they were.

You attended a Christmas open house at Donald and Eugene's. They had the ten-foot tree with a mountain of wrapped gifts beneath, the house decked out in red and green. The spiral-cut honey baked ham. A former Broadway actor and singer playing "Have Yourself a Merry Little Christmas" on a grand piano. It might almost have been sweetly traditional if 90 percent of the guests had not been gay.

You'd already been to a couple of AA meetings in this new town, and someone had told you that Donald was in the program, though you hadn't bumped into him there. And you hadn't known that about him, but then you didn't know Donald and Eugene all that well. At least you thought it was Donald this someone had referred to. And you thought so even more strongly when he put an arm around your shoulder to offer you a drink, and said, "The eggnog is non-alcoholic."

So you followed him into the kitchen, where a pretty, young, obviously gay man—hired as a waiter for the evening—arranged a tray of spinach canapés in puff pastry to circulate among the guests. You followed Donald into the kitchen because you knew him, because you needed to know somebody there. And you asked him if he was a friend of Bill W.'s. But you knew right off he wasn't, because he called Eugene over from the oven and said, "Gene, do we know somebody named Bill W.?"

Eugene laughed and said he'd explain it to him later, and then you knew it was Eugene. Eugene was in the program. And then you felt a little better because now you knew that about each other.

Later you clustered around the Christmas tree with them, and with a striking woman with a shock—no a mass, no a waterfall—of white hair, conversing just loudly enough to be heard over the piano and the caroling. Eugene explained to Donald what that meant. The kind of signal it is, when you ask someone if he knows Bill W. And Donald laughed and made reference to "knowing Dorothy," which was a new one on you; nobody really explained it, either, but it seemed clear in context that if you know Dorothy, it means you're gay.

And meanwhile this woman, she'd taken some sort of interest in you, which made you a bit vigilant. You were not the only straight person there, but it was an interesting lesson on life in the minority. And though you were not exactly flummoxed by this woman's attention, you did begin to fast-forward in your head to the time in the evening you might need to address it, correct her assumption about you. Then you noticed she wore a wedding ring, a traditional set with a diamond engagement ring and a gold band, which confused you. Because the ring and her focus on you— her sort of figurative leaning into you—represented two halves of a reality which added up to a whole you couldn't understand. So you felt one had to be false, yet there they both were. And you didn't like thinking about things that left you confused like that, still don't, never have. So you stopped thinking.

Later you stood out on the upstairs patio, looking, from what seemed like miles above the scene, at the creek spilling into the ocean. And she came out and stood with you, just like you knew she would. You surprised yourself a little, didn't you, when you realized you knew she would? Then you wondered whether you'd wanted her to, somehow invited her to, but you couldn't imagine how. Or why. Curiosity, maybe. Just to sort it all out. But it didn't feel like that; it felt like you'd courted the attention and now here it was, leaving you wondering what to do with it. How many times in your life had you invited something, and then gotten it, and then wondered what to do with it?

You opened your mouth to offer some kind of small talk, but never got that far. You knew you should have known better. She doesn't do small talk, and you shouldn't either.

"So, do you?" she asked.

And you had no idea "do you" what.

"Do I what?" you said.

And she said, "Know Dorothy."

It occurred to you then that you might have practiced more. Brought more mental preparation to the moment, since you knew damn well it was coming. Because the way it played out, you came off flustered, which undermined your intention to prove her incorrect.

"Who, me?" you said. "No. No, no. Not me. No." You listened to yourself, critiquing as you went along, knowing one "no" means no, three or four mean you're on the defensive for some reason. So you tried to patch it over by saying even more. "Me, no, I suppose I've led a bit of a sheltered life. I haven't met Dorothy. No."

She leaned in a little closer before she answered you, and you felt it coming, and it was already too late. You couldn't guess what her exact words would be, but you felt what you'd incited. You had done something to allow her to say what she said next to you, or at very least, failed to do something which might have prevented it. But what any of those somethings were lay beyond your reach, lie beyond your reach to this very day. So your helplessness was not merely complete but ongoing.

She said it to you because you let her.

"I could introduce you."

You left the door open just a crack, knowing even then that she is not the sort of woman who waits patiently in the hall.

3. Excuse Gary

Gary says, "I suppose your dog could sleep in the garage."

But of course you know he can't. He's too old and arthritic, and he'll howl if he doesn't know where you are. If he can't stay with you, you can't stay here. So you'll have to walk farther in the storm, only that's not good for Tully, either. Maybe you could sleep in the garage with him. Then you remember what just happened to your own garage, and you realize that sleep is not even on the menu for tonight.

You stand in the foyer, still holding Tully between your knees, holding his head so he won't shake off. Laura reappears with a stack of towels, one for your dog, two or three for you.

You say, "Maybe you could drive me to a hotel, then. Or call me a cab? Do we have cabs in this town?" It makes you feel so inadequate, not to know. It makes you feel so helpless to suddenly lose your electricity, your phone, and your car. It makes you feel so helpless to be so helpless.

"What's this, then?" Laura says, looking to Gary to see what he's done to you.

"My dog is old," you say by way of explanation. "He needs to stay warm. I need to keep him with me."

"Well, of course he'll be with you," Laura says. "You can sleep in the guest room. I'll make him a nice comfortable bed on the rug."

"The cats," Gary says.

"My dog is too old to chase cats."

You let the poor guy out from between your knees finally. Tent a towel over him and let him shake off into it. Then he unbalances himself, because his back legs and hips are not too steady. He falls into an off-kilter sit, nicely proving your point.

"He'll be fine, Gary," Laura says, and Gary goes upstairs.

Laura draws you a hot bath with bubbles. She lights candles in the bathroom. The windows steam as she towels your hair. You think it might be possible to get warm again. The bathroom door is open a crack for Tully to see in, to trust that he knows where you are. But it works both ways; you can see him, too, his boxy, gun-metal gray face poking in, his eyes blinking, his ears draped on the linoleum, and it makes you feel warmer.

You peel off your clothes, which are wet even though you wore your slicker. And you leave them in a wet, cold pile and climb into the steaming hot water and lean back and close your eyes. Laura sits on the floor on the bath mat, one hand trailing into your bath water. Trailing against your now-warm thigh. You wonder where Gary is now; what are the chances of him coming down here? You want to worry about that, but you can't hold your worry there for long.

You tell Laura everything. You tell her about the pine tree that crashed down on your deck. How you tried to look out to see the damage it had done, but there were no street lights, no moon. The flashlight couldn't show enough. Masses of pine needles. A splintered railing. And the breakfast room was starting to rain; that and the noise told you it was settling, pulling the deck away from the house. You tell her how afraid you were that next time it settled it might pull that whole room off your rented house. So you got in the car to go. But the garage door wouldn't open, not even manually. So you and Tully walked around the front and saw the second downed tree, the one that clipped the corner of the garage, buckled it and bent the garage door. Its trunk lay blocking your driveway anyway, so it didn't much matter whether you could open the garage or not. You tell her you would have gone to a motel if you had any way of getting there, but the phone lines were down—

She won't let you continue. She places a finger in front of your lips, holds your apologies captive there while she tells you, "Don't you dare think of coming anywhere but here. I wouldn't hear of it."

Then for long while you don't talk, either one of you, which feels better.

Laura changes her mind about the guest room. "You'll freeze." she says. "Our heater is gas but the thermostat is electric. That's why we have the wood stove going."

Which is why the house glows. You like her house glowing, but you wish she'd stop saying "our" and "we."

Together you pull the futon pad off onto the floor. Pull it over near the stove. Tully climbs onto it and Laura says nothing about that, so you don't, either. You're wearing a nightgown that smells like her, but you can't tell if it's a subtle perfume, or a soap, or just her. But you know Laura when you smell her. You lie down, listening to the wind howl and whistle, and she brings blankets, and covers you. And covers your dog.

She lies down beside you, and you think again about Gary upstairs: this time your worry sticks, right on that place. So you say it out loud. Just that one word.

"Gary."

"He won't come down," she says. You are about to ask why not, how she can be so sure he won't, but as usual she gives you no time to travel there. "He doesn't want to know."

So now you know for sure that he knows. Because you have to know something before you can know that you don't want to know it.

While you're thinking about this, a long-haired black cat walks into the room, spots Tully, arches his hack and freezes that way, hissing. Tully does what Tully always does. Nothing. Other than to wag his stumpy tail against the blanket.

While you're watching this happen, still half thinking about Gary, where he is and what he knows, you feel her lips brush sensitive places on your neck. Laura knows where to find those places, too. She knew where to look that very first night. By now she has them charted, memorized, prioritized. You want to push her away, because of Gary, but you don't push her away, because you don't want to. So instead you weave your hands into all that amazing hair and admit to yourself that you sought this out tonight, came here for precisely this reason.

Then Tully looks up, which makes Laura look up, and you hate to feel left out, so you look up, too. Gary is standing in the living room, looking down on all three of you, a glass of milk in one hand, a small plate in the other. You can't see what's on the plate because he's above you. But you hope there's really something on the plate. You hope he really came down to make himself real food, not just to come down. Not because he really does want to know.

You can see his face surprisingly well in the firelight, and you expect it to be hard, or cold, or angry, or forbidding, or shocked. No, not shocked. You knew he wouldn't be that. But he doesn't appear to be any of it. It's almost as if it's gone too far for all that. As if it's too late to feel all that now.

He says only two words, and he says them in a voice both quiet and polite, but you can't get those two words out of your head. Already you know they'll keep you awake all night, and in the morning you'll lie and say it was the wind. But it will have been those two words.

What he says is, "Excuse me."

Then he goes back upstairs.

4. Intruders

In the morning you open your eyes, surprised because you slept. Surprised that the wind let you sleep. Not to mention those words. You lie still a moment, stroking Tully's silky gray ears. You look up to see Laura looking in from the kitchen at you. Then you remember that she followed him upstairs last night. Left you and went up after him, and you were amazed at how much that hurt you. And now, looking back, you're amazed at how much it still hurts you now.

"Good, you're awake," she says. "Don't be startled if you hear me shouting."

She disappears again.

She begins shouting, and it startles you. "Get out!"

she screams. "You're not welcome here! Get the hell out of my house!"

Tully's head snaps up. A calico cat skitters out of the kitchen, spots Tully, panics, and runs upstairs. You wait, frozen, wondering what you're supposed to do. Laura sticks her head out again and smiles at you.

"You're startled," she says. She seems disappointed in you, which is the last thing you want Laura to be. "I told you not to be."

"Who are you shouting at?"

"The ants."

"Ants?"

"Yes. Ants."

"Is it ant season?"

"No. It's the damnedest thing. Isn't this weather bizarre? There's coffee."

Now she is gone again. You look out the window, and notice it's not raining. The wind has died off. You get up and stretch, and wish you had something to wear besides this nightgown; you don't wear nightgowns, and it doesn't feel right on you. Then you look down at the end of the futon pad and see your clothes—your jeans, and the big dark red corduroy shirt you appropriated from your ex-husband—clean and dry and fluffy and folded, waiting for you. So you put them on. Right there in the living room. As you do you wonder yet again where Gary is, but it doesn't seem like he could possibly walk in on anything more revealing than he already has.

He said excuse me.

You join Laura in the kitchen, tell her you'd love coffee, but of course she's already poured you a big mug. In fact, it has a nice amount of half-and-half in it, and you struggle for some memory of ever having told her how you take your coffee. It's too early for this. You sit down. She's wiping the counters, still in her nightgown, her solid hips rocking against the thin fabric. A light scatter of ants dash around near her sink, but they appear disorganized, as though they were just leaving.

"Do they leave when you yell at them?"

"Usually. I guess they don't want to be out in this weather any more than we do."

Tully bumps hard into your knee and then plunks down with a sigh. He's so old, poor Tully. You just know he's going to go off and leave you soon. Then what will you have? You look back up at Laura.

"Where's Gary?" Excuse me. That's what he said.

"He went over to your house."

"My house?"

"Yes, he took his chainsaw and drove over."

For a moment you have a vision of him wreaking vengeance on your innocent house with his chainsaw. "Why did he do that?"

"I asked him to."

You realize, to your disappointment, that you can't stay here with her. You want to, but you can't. You have to go home and assess your damages. You have to report your phone lines down, call your landlord. You have to see in the daylight how you'll ever get your car out of the garage. And, in the midst of all this, you have to face Gary.

Gary, holding a chainsaw.

5. Gary's Hands

He doesn't stop when you and Tully walk up. Maybe he doesn't see you. Or maybe he sees you, but he just doesn't stop. He certainly couldn't have heard you come up, not over the roar of that chainsaw. The weather is damp, chilly, but sunny and calm. A downed power line drapes partway across the street; you cut a wide arc around it and force Tully to do the same, though you doubt it's live. He's cutting up the tree that lies across your driveway. Slicing it into rounds and then moving the rounds off onto your lawn. Both your lawn and your driveway are now blanketed with pine needles and damp sawdust. He looks up at you, but still doesn't stop.

Excuse me.

This is the first you've seen him in broad daylight, and he's not what you were expecting somehow. You wonder if he'd say the same of you. He's younger than you thought. Younger than her, like yourself. He looks a bit rough, like a tradesman, like someone who would work construction. Like someone who is right at home cutting up a fallen tree with a chainsaw. Maybe you expected him to be more intellectual. Maybe you are surprised that she is married to a man who works with his hands. Maybe you are thinking all this to avoid thinking that you are still surprised she is married to a man.

You move close to him, within a foot or two, close enough to be heard over the chainsaw. It feels like a direct gamble with your safety and well-being but you do it anyway.

"Gary," you say. Nice and loud.

He cuts the power on the chainsaw. The silence resonates, bounces off pine trees, echoes out through the woods. He's wearing clear plastic goggles, and he raises them, as if he can't hear with them on. But he doesn't seem interested in hearing.

"Gary, I—

"Good, you're here," he says. "Grab the other end of that limb."

You do. And you work together like that for five, ten minutes, during which you do not find the nerve to address him again.

A pair of your neighbors strolls by. An older couple. They have a poodle on a leash, and Tully rambles unsteadily out into the street to sniff at it.

"Is he friendly?" they call.

You nod, because you've lost the feel for talking.

"My, you really took some damage," the wife says.

"Wasn't that a lulu?" the husband adds. "Been in this town 30 years, never saw anything like it."

You get the impression that they have come out walking for just this reason: because there is damage everywhere, and they want to see it and comment.

Enamored with their poodle, Tully tries to follow them away. You call his name sharply and he lumbers back to you. Then, having found your voice again, you say, "Gary. I—"

"Tully," he says, "I used to work with a guy named Tully. Built a house three streets over from here with him. What made you name your dog Tully?"

You explain to him that your dog's name is actually Jethro Tull, and that he will respond to any or all parts

63

of that name, but you rarely call him Jethro, for fear that people will think you are a fan of—rather than the immortal rock band—the Beverly Hillbillies. Gary nods thoughtfully, as if this requires deep consideration.

This time you've only just opened your mouth to speak, haven't even gotten to the "Gary" part yet, when he overspeaks you. "Unlock the front door, and I'll go through and see if I can open your garage door. I doubt it, though. I think you'll have to have it taken out."

The landlord will have to have it taken out, you think. The joys of a rented home.

You let him in, but don't immediately follow. Instead you stand outside surveying the house for a minute or two. You look closely at the corner of the garage, which is structurally damaged, cracked and slightly buckled. You wonder if a new door can be installed in this mess. Then you let that be the landlord's problem.

You find Gary inside the garage. It's nicely dim in there, which seems to help.

"Gary—" you say.

"No luck on this. Sorry. I tried. I'm going out on your back deck, and I'm going to cut up as much of that tree as I can and throw it into the lot behind you. The more weight I can take off for now the better."

He brushes by you and disappears.

You stand frozen a moment too long, one hand on the roof of your useless car. Then you realize you don't know where Tully is, so you go through the house looking. He's in the breakfast room, watching Gary set up on your back deck. Watching him break branches away to make a spot to stand. You watch, too, for a while. You watch his hands, which look broad and square and rough, and you try to imagine them on her full, soft-yet-solid body. But you soon realize that you not only can't imagine that, you want badly not to.

Excuse me. As if he were the one to be forgiven.

You decide that to say "Gary" again would be a mistake. You decide to say something different and fast, and then go away and leave him alone, because he so wants you to, and he's asked so nicely so many times.

"It's nice of you to do this," you say, before he even knows you're behind him.

"Laura asked me to."

You wonder, briefly, why people always do what Laura asks them to. You know they do, but you wonder why. You wonder whether, if Laura asked you to do something nice for Gary, something you didn't want to do, didn't feel you owed it to him to do, would you?

While you're wondering this, Gary says, "Did you call telephone repair service? Before you left our house?"

"No. I didn't." You're ashamed to admit you planned to come back here and do it, because you're so used to having utilities, you just couldn't make the mental jump into understanding that you currently don't. "I'll go do that now."

You leave Tully home, to keep Gary company, and you know Gary won't mind. Because Tully won't say Gary's name in that tone that alerts him of more information to follow.

6. The Last Puzzle Piece

The phone company keeps you on hold for a long time, during which Laura stands over you combing her fingers through your hair, firmly massaging your scalp. It feels wonderful, yet it seems essential you not admit or even betray that. The music they play while you hold is beginning to irritate you.

"What about the fact that you're hurting him?" you say. You expect her hands to leave your hair, but they don't. They don't even stop massaging. You can't throw Laura off her stride.

"I didn't realize his interests were yours."

Neither did you. And you don't know if you've suddenly discovered that you do care about him, or if that was only a diversionary tactic.

"What about the fact that you're hurting me?" you say, which seems more to the point.

"I didn't know I was."

"You think I don't have feelings?"

"I thought you weren't taking this all that seriously."

You might have thought that yourself, for a minute. Early on. But it was a ludicrous minute, anyway.

"If you're gay, what are you doing with him?"

Without missing a beat, without taking her hands out of your hair, she says, "If you're straight, what are you doing with me?"

Of course, you just hate it when she answers a question with another question, and you tell her so, in no uncertain terms.

But she says, "No." She says, "No. what you really hate is when I ask questions you have no answers for."

And she's maddeningly correct, as always. Well, it's both. But it's true you have no answer for that. And, really, you've asked yourself the question a lot lately. You would think that, however rudimentary, you'd have dredged up some sort of theory by now.

A real voice comes on the line, so you report your phone trouble. You want to tell the woman all my lines are down, all over my life, come fix me, but you know she only cares about your phone service. While you're talking, Laura apparently grows bored by the digression, and wanders off into the kitchen.

When you've hung up the phone, you sit still a moment with all your irritation, and it's so damn familiar. Such a familiar frustration. It's the familiarity that jogs you to see. It's that successful jigsaw puzzle feeling, like finally remembering where you've met someone before. You follow Laura's path into the kitchen. She's wiping her counters again; about six ants still haven't left, so you brace yourself in case she's about to shout at them.

"I do know the answer to that question," you say.

"Yes. So do I." You want her to be wrong, to strike way out in left field, but of course she beans you a direct hit. "You thought it would be completely different, almost by design. That you couldn't possibly find yourself right back in the same pattern of relationship again."

She looks over her shoulder and smiles at you, a little sadly, you think. Then she sweeps over to put her arms around you, and the whole time she's sweeping you think, I'm not going to let her hold me, but then, when she arrives, you do. You even hold her in reply.

But it's really not very different. Is it?

You want to tell her the only real difference—as far as you can see—is that the sex makes you feel inept. Even though you've only had a small handful of instances by which to judge. You want to tell her that you shouldn't have to lose your virginity twice, that it was hard enough to learn how to please a man, that you're a grown woman and this sudden rookie status demeans you. But you don't tell her any of that. In fact, you don't tell her anything. She tells you.

She says, "Okay. I'm not going to hold you in something that isn't working for you."

But you want her to hold you. You hate this part. There's the letting go, and then, ten times worse, the being let go of. This is another obvious repetition of pattern: she's right, this isn't working, you have no future here together, but you still don't want to be let go. That's the part that feels like dying.

You let go, take a step back from her. You made it through your divorce, and you didn't die, did you? So that feeling is not exactly what it seems.

You walk home, hoping Gary will be gone now.

You get your wish. He is. Sometimes you get what you need.

At least now, next time someone asks if you've met this Dorothy person, you won't be caught all vulnerable and stupid. You'll be able to say, hey, I wasn't just dropped on this planet yesterday. I know a few things.

But no one ever asks you that again. Maybe because you never invite anyone to.

THE EXPATRIATE

Dear Drew,

I heard about what happened, what you tried to do. Bertha told me. Do you even remember her? She is one of the few who knows of some connection between us, which is to say, she knows I want to hear news. Even those few people really don't know, though. Or if they know, they don't know they know. Or, if they know they know, they have been decent enough not to put it all over the province. Bertha said you couldn't have been serious or you would have put the gun in your mouth. But I remember everything you told me, including where you said you would go to do it, which is just where she said you did go, and about not wanting the person who found you to come onto something grisly. I loved you for that, I wonder if you know. I loved you because you were crazy enough to kill yourself and considerate enough not to want to ruin anyone's day in the process. You don't meet a man like that every day.

News travels fast. You were still doing your time in the hospital when I heard. I should have come to see you, like I should have come to Audrey's funeral. I guess I'm writing this to say I would have if I could. I guess if I could I wouldn't need to write this.

Steven has me seeing a good psychologist now. Did I tell you that, last time I wrote? Because it was his suggestion, I feel a little more comfortable with the whole deal. He makes it sound like a reasonable thing to do. He says I'm in remarkable mental health all things considered. He has that nice calm, reasonable way. He can make a thing like that sound good. Positive somehow. Maybe you would prefer I talked less about Steven. But then I guess since you won't be reading this it doesn't matter. Bobbi says that when I write these letters I should say what I want to say, not what I think you want to hear. Which I can do, knowing I will never send them.

Bobbi is my new psychologist, in case I forgot to mention that. I never talk to Steven about you. He doesn't even know there is such a thing as you. Oh, I guess he's heard of you, like most people around here have, but not in connection with me. Bobbi says it's okay to feel the way I still do about you, that I need to vent that rather than stifle it. As long as I don't follow through, whatever I feel is okay. A huge relief, because stifling it never worked at all. I think all these years I was mostly waiting for someone to give me permission to stop.

Because of what didn't happen between us, not because of what did, that's why I can't let go, I think. Because we never took that final step. It's such a big piece of unfinished business. We brushed so close so many times it was like years of foreplay. Well, not even like it. It was. Sometimes I think, just one time, just so I can say we finally did after all these years. But Bobbi is pretty sure it wouldn't stop there. I'm lying, actually, when I make up reasons why I can't let go. I don't know why. I might just be wired that way. Maybe even Bobbi can't change that. Maybe Steven can write checks to her until I die and she still won't have changed that. I tell him the sessions are going really well.

She says it's even okay to have those weak moments when I realize that you never meant me any harm. But then she adds that I have to accept that you will do harm just the same. When I'm feeling weak I need to call her or see her and be told that again. I don't forget, exactly. I just forget why it seemed so true.

Steven makes me happy. I think I say that too much. I have to tell you though, since you will never read this, that when it comes to sex, it only works when I think about you. Bobbi says what I have with Steven is real love which is a lot harder to feel. She says I've been desensitized and I need more drama. Like when your taste buds are weak you need hot spicy food. I figure by now an atomic device would have to explode underneath me to get me to feel. Which is pretty much what you were. In my life anyway.

There, I wrote all that down and you know what? I don't feel better. I've been doing this for nine days and I don't feel different. She says keep doing it though, even so. Keep writing letters, keep burning them. These things take time.

I'll always love you Drew. You know that. Maybe if you didn't know, then it would be safe to see you. But you do.

Love,
Jane

She folds the letter carefully into thirds, leaving a half-inch paper border at the top, to grasp it by as it comes out of the envelope. Even though she knows it never will. Because this is common courtesy, and because Bobbi has told her never to act as if she will not mail the letters. Then she remembers mentioning in the letter that she would not mail it, which might negate the whole purpose. She struggles with this, but decides not to rewrite it. It took a lot out of her the first time.

In a careful hand she writes Drew's full name on the envelope, and his address, which she knows by heart. Then her own return address in the corner.

Why do I put it in an envelope and address it? she asked Bobbi at first.

Because when we decide not to send a letter, we crumple it up and throw it in the fireplace. This is more like really sending it. Symbolically. You get it all ready like you'll really send it, but you use the fireplace for a mailbox. It's all very symbolic.

Jane follows Bobbi's directions carefully, even though she does not wholeheartedly believe what Bobbi says. She has made an on-faith decision to follow directions. For Steven. She reminds herself that she does not wholeheartedly believe in anything, except those things she shouldn't, like Drew.

She licks the edge of the envelope flap and seals it shut.

The phone rings. It is one of Steven's credit card companies. Well, equally theirs, she supposes, although Steven opened the account. The woman wants her to purchase protection against disability or involuntary unemployment. Jane listens to a speech about the plan, which will make payments for them in such an emergency, because the woman went to the trouble to memorize it. When it's Jane's turn to talk, she's not sure how people with credit cards think, what choices they make. She never used to use them, and they haven't been married long. She suggests the woman call back later, when Steven is home.

A split second after she hangs up the phone, he comes through the door.

She fixes dinner, they eat, and she asks about his day. He is an engineer. He works in an office until a bridge support weakens or a sewer line ruptures. Then he stands out In The Field, as he calls it, in a parka with the hood up, warming his hands on a coffee cup and talking to men standing beside heavy equipment, which idles loudly as they talk. If she asks, he will tell her all about his day. She always asks.

Jane has read books and seen movies containing

men who hold jobs as engineers. They bring home good paychecks with health benefits and retirement plans, and they do this for decades and don't mind. Until Steven she had never really known one up close, so had always suspected they were a kind of archetypal legend, like the happy family. Every time she asks, she expects him to say he minds now and can't do it anymore. He never does.

After dinner they do the dishes together, and Steven sits down to pay the monthly bills. Jane watches and asks herself if she is happy. Because she knows she should be at a moment like this, which compels her to test the response. When she is at a picnic or a softball game with Steven's family, she asks herself if she is having fun. She knows they are, and also that when people have fun they probably don't ask.

He puts on his hooded parka and drives to the post office with the bill payments. He likes the sense of completion.

She tucks into bed with a book.

When he comes back, he strips and climbs in with her. The skin on his face is cold and stubbly with five o'clock shadow and he seems to want to make love. While they are making love, she remembers that she forgot to tell him about the call from the credit card lady. It doesn't seem worth interrupting him now. Then she remembers the promise she made to herself. Not to think about Drew this time. Just as she breaks it.

Half an hour after he drops off to sleep, which she knows by his breathing, she sits up, remembering. She turns on the light.

"What?" he says, which he always says when

wakened.

"I left a letter on the table. I forgot. I'll go get it."

"Oh, that," he says, still very sleepy. "I mailed that."

"You did? It didn't have a stamp."

"I put a stamp on it and mailed it. Didn't you want me to? It was on the table."

"No, that's fine. Just so I know. Where it went."

She turns off the light and Steven goes back to sleep.

Steven is gone to work by six-thirty a.m. Jane dresses warmly and goes out back to tend the horses.

Ephraim comes to the fence to greet her, his hooves clumping on the frozen ground, puffing great clouds of warm steam from his nostrils. She scratches his upper lip, the way he likes. He is an enormous chestnut, a Dutch Warmblood, huge muscular legs with prominent veins like a human bodybuilder, and a Roman nose. He wears a warm blanket. He is hers. He always has been.

The boarder horse, a bay Arab mare half Ephraim's size, stays behind in the three-sided shelter, front legs splayed, indulging her neuroses by rocking her long neck back and forth. Jane is considering asking the boarders to take the Arab elsewhere, because they don't take care of her.

She uses a hay hook to break up and drag away the crust of ice on the watering trough, so they can drink. The water seems murky with algae again. Steven, who knows nothing about horses, doesn't think it's a problem; the man who delivers the hay, who knows quite a lot, agrees. Drew knows everything about horses. If he were here, he'd tell her to clean it. "When you love a horse you take care of him." So today she will bail out the freezing trough, scrub it clean and allow it to fill again, frostbitten fingers or no.

Ephraim leans into the fence, pressing his massive forehead against her, and she wraps her arms around his head, enjoying his warmth. Ephraim knows Drew well, is the only living soul in her life who does, so she discusses Drew often.

"It's not even seven a.m.," she says. "So it's still sitting there in the mailbox. It won't even go out until twelve-thirty. But it's gone, anyway, Ephraim. Once it's in that box, it belongs to the Postal Service. There's no way to get it back that I know of. Maybe it doesn't matter now. Watch for Drew, anyway. He'll be coming right down that driveway I think. Maybe he'll get it tomorrow. I wonder how long it'll take him to come. You do think he'll come, don't you?"

The Arab wanders up, tentatively, and Jane realizes they want to eat. She separates off two big flakes of alfalfa hay and tips them over the fence into their feeders. Ephraim gently pulls the corners off his. The Arab grabs the flake by the top, lifts it out of the feeder and shakes it, raising a flurry of alfalfa particles. She drops the hay on the frozen ground and eyes it sideways, as if it frightens her by being there.

Jane turns her back on the horses and looks to the driveway, imagining the crunch of gravel, thinking how that same driveway will look when it is no longer empty.

Two days later, while she is trying hard not to think like a waiting person, she hears Ephraim whinny his excited greeting. Her heart pounds, and it makes her dizzy, wondering if Drew will be there when she opens the back door.

He is faced away from her, scratching Ephraim's upper lip. A new silver Cadillac idles in the driveway, sending steam clouds of exhaust into the gray afternoon. He's wearing a plaid shirt, no coat, and his hair is longer. It hangs straight over the back of his collar. She steps out and he turns around. He still wears black sunglasses, even in winter.

She walks to him. He puts on that twisted little smile, probably not on purpose. She knows that if she could see his eyes they would be soft. She knows they can be strong and frightening and cold, but she won't see that come out today. She knows where to go and where not to go, not to see that come out.

She touches the sleeve of his shirt. "You'll freeze."

"You know I wouldn't have come by. You know that, right? If you hadn't written."

"Why didn't you wear a jacket, silly?"

He touches the sleeve of her sweater, as if to remind her that she is similarly underdressed. The pair of simple touches conveys an almost unbearable heaviness.

She tries to swallow. "You didn't come by before you did it. I couldn't imagine you wouldn't come say goodbye first." She wants him to say it was for her sake.

"I did come by, three times. I just didn't come in. I promised you, after you got married."

She wishes he hadn't mentioned promises.

"You must be doing great," she says, pointing with her chin to the idling Cadillac.

Money was never Drew's strong suit. Maybe Audrey left him money. Life insurance, maybe. They walk to the car together, get in and slam the doors. The heater is running full blast.

"I've had it for two months. I didn't put anything down. First month was payment-free. Don't ask me how I rate all that credit. I haven't figured it out myself." He tilts his head and his dark hair parts, falls over the corner of his sunglasses, and shields half his face. He seems puzzled and curious.

"How much are the payments?"

"Nine hundred a month."

"How can you make that?"

"I can't." They listen to the heater blow for a few protracted moments. Through the snowy windshield Ephraim runs the fence, whinnying for Drew. "I didn't figure I'd be around."

She nods, remembering. She reaches out and taps his knee lightly. "Are you glad now that you didn't die?"

"No." It takes a long time to say, as if it had a lot of syllables. "I'm already planning my next one." He looks up at her and smiles, like it hurts him in a wonderful way to see her. "I wouldn't have come except. . ."

She nods. She knows. "I hope you don't really do it. But you have to come say goodbye if you do."

"You won't try to talk me out of it?"

"Of course I will. If I can."

"That's the problem with talking to somebody beforehand."

"Doesn't have to be beforehand."

"Well, I can't very well do it after." He laughs at his own joke, maybe thinking she will laugh too.

"I don't know. I'm not sure. You hear about things like that. I had a friend once who said she was lying in bed one night, and she felt like somebody was in the room. It didn't feel scary, though. And then later she found out this guy she used to date had just died."

She watches his reaction. He shrugs, then nods.

"Well, then we'd know," she says, "if you can do that or not." She wants to be the person who'd still matter enough, even after he died, to warrant a stop. "This car is incredible."

He brags about the horsepower, which seems odd. He didn't used to care about things like that. She remembers a man at a horse show bragging that his car had 180 horsepower. Drew was riding by on Candle, and he said that sounded like 179 horses more than necessary, to this man he'd never seen.

He shows her all the power features, such as the seat which automatically adjusts to three pre-set positions. He points out the CD. player, but says he has no CDs and asks if she does. She says she and Steven still use cassettes. The inside of the car goes cavernous and quiet at the mention of his name.

After a while he says, "We should go for a drive sometime. Soon. Before they come take this back."

Bobbi is in her head, feeding her lines. Say, It's all in the past, Drew. I'm happily married now. Say, I know what a drive actually means, in our shared language. Say, I'm not as good at self-destructive behavior as I used to be. But if she had wanted Bobbi's advice, she would have called Bobbi when the letter was accidentally mailed. Bobbi probably would have said, There are no accidents.

"Let's do it now," she says. Before I change my mind.

He asks her if she wants to get anything out of the house, like a coat, or leave a note or anything. She says no.

Drew's farm is more than a hundred kilometers south, off Highway 2, almost halfway to Toronto. An icy wind off the lake blows snow sideways across the road, which hasn't been plowed. But the Cadillac has an advanced traction control system, he says, and good snow tires. He says he needs to stop home to feed the dogs.

As they pull onto his property she sees changes. Sad changes. Audrey's little plane is sitting out in a pasture, half-covered by a drift of snow. Not the one she crashed. The one she was building in the back of the barn. Jane heard it was ninety percent finished when she died. The house looks old and tired, like no one loves it anymore. Drew parks by the barn.

"Wouldn't it be better for that inside?" she says.

"Better for what?"

"The plane."

"Oh, that. I guess." He seems distracted, as though he has to go far away to consider it. "A guy came by to look at it. He didn't buy it. I never hauled it back in."

They step out into the freezing air, and he pulls the barn door open, shaking his hand briskly after touching the metal handle. Three dogs come to greet him, old Mister the hound, who she knows, but who is now unbelievably, painfully old, then two skinny black and white Border Collies, big pups, strangers. Drew closes the barn door behind them, turns on fluorescent overhead lights. He takes down a twenty-five pound bag of dry dog food, tears it open and sets it on its side, spilling kibble into the barn aisle. He refills a horse-size watering bucket from the hose tap. The dogs ignore the food and wag around his legs. She looks at the mountain of kibble and doesn't ask how long he thinks they'll be gone.

Wandering up the barn aisle, she is a student again, a teenager, because she always was, here. She feels short and unattractive and insubstantial. She hurries past the stairs leading up to the loft, her old home.

Every stall is empty, bedded in clean straw and shavings, canvas web doors clipped across the open entryways, as if each stall expects a horse again soon. At the end of the barn aisle stands his shelf of trophies. His ribbons are mounted on the wall, including his Olympic Silver, and a photo of him accepting it with the other two members of the Canadian team. She received the same photo in the mail when she wrote him a fan letter at the age of fourteen. And the photo of him taking Candle over a seven foot one jump, the horse seeming to drop straight down, back legs kicked out and up to keep from knocking the rail. She'd been sitting in the stands that day, at the International Horse Show in Buffalo. She has not since seen or even heard of a horse and rider going higher than seven one. Only Drew on Candle had a clean final round.

She turns to see that he's done, and watching her

patiently.

"Nothing you haven't seen."

"Where are all your horses?"

"Sold them or gave them away."

"Candle?" You sold Candle?

He shakes his head, and she knows. "He was old. His arthritis was so bad, I couldn't ask him to do another winter. It would have been selfish. You know how athletes are. Our bodies fall apart on us. The school horses I gave away, mostly to the students. I kept wondering why nobody figured out what I was going to do. Or maybe they did, but they didn't care."

He slides the barn door open and motions her through. She asks about the plan for the dogs, and he says his neighbor promised to take care of them if anything ever happened to him. He opens the car door for her and asks if she wants him to go into the house and get her a coat. She says no, it's warm in the car, which is where they'll be. She wants to leave. The barn makes her feel young and Audrey's plane seems to be staring at her. The gravel driveway crunches as they pull away.

He asks where she'd like to go. She suggests they cross the border. She hasn't been to The States in years.

They stop at the Falls on the Canadian side, at her request. It's a mistake, she realizes almost immediately, because it's a longish tramp from the parking lot to any good viewing sight, and they're not dressed for the cold. It's that early winter dusk, and when they reach a railing, it's too fogged in to see the falls. She hears them, though, and feels the cold mist of them, and Drew puts an arm around her shoulder to keep her warm.

She can tell that his pain is setting in again. His medication must be wearing off. She's watched this for years, though she realizes he also has a gunshot wound now. She doesn't know where, or how much it hurts him, only that he miraculously missed almost everything important.

When they get back to the car he starts the engine and runs the heater. She asks. It still hurts, he says. But it's nothing compared to his back, after all these years.

Then he tells her something she didn't know about the self-inflicted gunshot. The round was supposed to explode on impact. As he explains, he takes his pill bottle out of the glove box and shakes three into his hand.

"So, what happened? It was just a dud?"

"I guess. You know I'm only good for twenty minutes of driving now." He swallows the pills without water.

"Go around," she says, and takes over the wheel.

It's not twenty minutes to The Peace Bridge, but he's already nodding, his lids heavy. The way she knows him best. The car feels huge and smooth, but strange, like driving a whole house. But also secure somehow. More familiar than it should.

As they drive through customs, she tells the border guard they are both Canadian citizens, which is only half true. She jabs Drew in the ribs because the guard has to hear it from him. He waves them through.

Darkness falls. She heads for Buffalo, for lack of another plan. She stops at a service station and calls Steven.

"Where are you?" he says.

"Niagara Falls."

"Your truck is here."

"I'm with a friend."

"When will you be home?"

"I'm not exactly sure." She marvels at her own lack of preparation for this inevitable exchange.

"Should I be worried about this?"

"I don't think so. It's just an old friend, whose head is in a bad place. I know, the blind leading the blind, right?"

"Stop it, Jane. I'm a little worried."

"Well, that's appropriate," she says. "But I really think it's going to be okay. If I'm not home tonight I'll probably be there when you get home from work tomorrow. Love you. Bye."

She hangs up quickly.

As she pulls into Buffalo, she feels disturbingly without destination. She wonders how long he'll sleep. She drives through downtown, just to see if it's changed. It has. She passes an open record store, pats her jeans pocket to see if she has money. She does, but doesn't think it's much, and wonders if Drew has money, and if she should save hers for food and gas.

She wanted to buy a CD, the one she has at home on cassette, with that song that reminds her of her time with Drew. "Why," it's called. She wanted him to hear the way the word "why" spins out into eleven syllables, the last one strangely long and modulated, like Drew saying no. Maybe he'd answer the question.

She gets off the expressway at Delaware Avenue and drives to the Buffalo Equestrian Club, because she's tired and sleepy and wants to stop. She pulls into the familiar rutted driveway, and parks by the office.

She watches him sleep until it seems scary to be where she can. Then she slips into the big back seat, and tries to get a night's sleep. And wants to be home. Every time the cold wakes her, she climbs into the front seat to run the heater.

She wakes up with Drew on top of her.

"Wake up," he says, "before you freeze."

But she doesn't feel cold, just his hands under her sweater, running up her rib cage, and his lips on her neck. She tries to draw a breath but it decides to be a gasp. He releases that sound into her ear, that she hasn't heard for years, and hasn't forgotten, and pushes against her.

They hear a car pull in and park beside them. They keep down until the footsteps disappear, then hear another car. They sit up. She feels half relieved for the interruption, because things just happen, with him, to a point, unless concrete circumstances prevent it.

She sits, adjusting her breathing, calming her heart rate by will. The building looms like a warehouse, like it always has, a mammoth arena hooded with windows in small, square panes, except now almost every one is broken. She looks at the car parked beside them and says, "Henry."

"Who?"

"Old Henry. The stable man."

"What about him?"

"He's still here. He's still driving the same car. I don't believe it."

They run shivering inside. Henry is turning on lights in the office, and the Tack and Gift Shoppe. He's grown shorter, and more stooped. He still carries himself with the subservience of a white plantation slave. He blinks at them.

"Morning."

"You don't remember me, Henry."

He moves close for a good look.

"Jane? Miss Jane? You sure did grow up!"

"I can't believe you're still here, Henry."

"Oh, I know a good thing when I see one."

She tries to imagine his cold, tedious job in that light. She starts to introduce Drew, but he waves that off.

"No introduction necessary. Pleasure to meet you again, Mr. Duncan. You two are gonna freeze. Where your coats? Hold on."

When he shuffles away, Drew says, "Did I meet him before?"

She points to the photo on the wall. The same one that hangs in his barn. Andrew Duncan on Candle Power clearing seven one. In this arena. Drew has come through this club on pro show circuits, maybe half a dozen times, unlike Jane, who grew up here, who learned to ride here. But as the most notable rider to come through, he is the most easily remembered.

Henry comes back with two clean, heavy horse

blankets, and they wrap up. Henry starts a pot of coffee, and Jane has to tell him what she's been doing for the last dozen years. Which she hates, because she figures she hasn't done much. Never made it to the Olympics. Never went pro. But then, she doesn't even have to ask what's new with him.

"Canada?" he says. "Why there? No offense, Mr. Duncan."

"None taken," he says, clearly fixated on the coffee drip.

"Needed the change of scene," she says, which sounds weak.

She never told Drew she followed him there, dropped everything when she read that after the accident he'd retired, and settled down to teach. Gave up her country of birth, and, well, really nothing else. She had nothing else worth keeping at the time. She told Drew only that she'd run away from home, another truth, one truth out of two. She doesn't want to tell Henry either one.

Holding styrofoam cups of strong black coffee, one hand peeking out under the huge padded flannel blankets, they step out into the boxes and sit, and watch a solitary young woman work her horse in the arena. Drew leans back and puts his feet up on the rail. He puts his black sunglasses on. His eyes are inordinately sensitive to light.

"Why are we here again?" he says quietly.

"I don't know. Where should we be?"

"I don't know." He sips coffee. "Alone somewhere?"

The woman reins her horse to a dirt-throwing stop right in front of them. She pats her horse's neck, above where the snug double reins have worked up a lather. "You look like Andrew Duncan," she says. She's irritatingly young.

"I am."

"Wow. I used to be a big fan of yours."

Drew shows no expression. Jane winces inwardly. It's almost as bad as the comment she initially feared. Didn't you used to be. . .? Then she says one more sentence, just as bad.

"I grew up watching you ride."

Drew gives her a nod and an imitation smile, and she squeezes the horse's sides and canters off. They watch her in silence as she shows off with dressage work. She is properly attired in jodhpurs and English boots and black hard hat, modified only by a down jacket. The horse is a leggy black, Morgan maybe, with his winter coat partially buzzed away. He looks freshly groomed, wearing leg tape and matching bell boots. And according to the clock in the arena, it's barely seven a.m. Which can only mean one thing. This girl is going to the Olympics. And Jane is not.

On each trip by she smiles at Drew. On one, she calls out, "I'm nervous now." She could do that and not be flirting, but she is flirting. Women do, with Drew. Sometimes they can't help it and sometimes they don't even know it, but they always do.

Jane looks up to the shattered windows. So much decay.

"Let's go," she whispers.

"Where?"

"Somewhere we can be alone."

He raises his eyebrows and follows her out. They

leave the blankets. Henry is not inside, so they don't say goodbye.

As Drew backs the Cadillac out of its parking space, she remembers what called her back to this place. Other than the fact that she grew up here, because her house was no place for such an activity.

"This is where we met, Drew. You probably don't remember."

"I thought we met in my barn."

"No, this was two years before that. Right by that stable entrance. You'd come down for the International. I followed you around all weekend. Everywhere but the men's room. I even followed you when you hot-walked Candle. I was fourteen. I thought you didn't even know I was there. Then all of a sudden you turned and spoke to me. Nearly stopped my heart."

"What did I say? Something witty and brilliant, I hope."

"You said, 'Want something to do, kid? Want to hot-walk my horse?' "

He smiles, hidden behind his dark glasses, the way she's used to seeing him. He doesn't remember. She knew he wouldn't.

She remembers that her hands shook when she took the reins from him, and that every three steps or so she reached a hand back to touch Candle, as if to verify his existence. She remembers the way his neck muscles felt, coiled under foamy sweat and thick, smooth-coated skin. She remembers Candle best from that first meeting. He was like Drew: big, powerful, a little scary.

"I was a little bit scared of you," she says out of

nowhere.

He reaches his hand out and places it on her thigh. "You didn't know me." He turns his hand palm up, and she runs her fingers along it. It feels cool and padded and soft.

She knows that could not have been why, because she's come to know him well over the years and she's a lot scared of him now.

Drew has money. Well, he has credit cards. She almost asks how he'll ever pay the bills, but she knows. Audrey kept them in good shape, now she's gone, they're out of control, and Drew doesn't expect to be around long enough to worry.

He stops at a discount drug store and she waits in the warm car while he buys toothbrushes and hairbrushes and toothpaste. Buy winter coats, she almost tells him. If she had one, she'd step out of the car now and find her own way home.

They sit in the car for a moment outside the hotel. Drew opens the drug store bag rather gingerly.

"Look," he says. "I'm no good at this. But I just thought. I don't know." He sets a box of condoms on the seat. "I thought you might want me to use these. Or I might want me to. I don't know."

She feels a tightness in her chest. "I didn't know. . ."

"What?"

"Nothing."

"No, what? You didn't know what?"

"That we were going for broke this time."

"Isn't that what you want? You said in the letter that's what you want."

"I also said it wouldn't stop there. That letter was never supposed to get to you. It got mailed by accident."

"There are no accidents," he says.

She thinks of the day he broke his back in a jumping competition, ending his career, and wonders if he believed that at the time. Or if he really believes it now. Or if he would if it didn't happen to serve him.

They take showers, Jane first, and she lies in bed naked and waits for him, which is nothing so unusual, because they've seen each other naked before. If Bobbi were here Jane would say, I know this looks like a step back, but I remember the bad times now, which I'm always saying I can't. And you're always saying I have to.

When he steps out of the bathroom she sees the toll a few years has taken, and the bullet wound. It's near the center of his chest. He sees her looking.

"I was aiming for my heart," he says. "But I missed."

"You always used to say you had no heart."

"Then maybe I'm not as bad a shot as I thought."

He eases himself under the covers. They lie quietly for a few uncomfortable minutes.

"What's wrong?" he says.

She sighs, overwhelmed by the vastness of the answer.

"Do you remember when I left your place, and I got a job in that racing stable?" Left him, she means, but this sounds better. "They had all these studs there. One of them, they never actually let him breed. They used him like a tester, to see if the mare was in heat. If she was they hauled him off and brought out one of the better stallions."

Maybe it's a mistake to talk about racing stables. Maybe it only reminds him of the three and a half years he spent in prison for beating a horse trainer to death, after the trainer "froze" the injured leg on a racehorse so many times that the bone snapped coming down the stretch. That was years before she met him, but she always saw it as a subject to avoid. One of many.

"Anyway, one day they decided to let him breed. The guys figured they'd give him a break. So he got up on this mare. And then he got down again." And she'd felt a tragic bond with the poor confused animal. She waits for some reaction.

"I take it there's a message here."

"Well, just that he got so used to thinking of sex as something that got interrupted."

"Who does the stud represent, you or me?"

"Never mind," she says. "Sorry I brought it up."

He picks up the box of condoms and throws it across the room, hard, and it bounces off the opposite wall. She knows he's angry. She knew he would be. She decides not to be scared this time, but it's a hard habit to break.

"You were the one who wanted it," he says.

"I wanted to marry you. I wanted you to love me. I didn't want you to sneak up to the loft and paw me and rub against me and disappear again."

"You never argued about it."

"No, I didn't. But I was aiming for your heart, you know?"

He lets out a snorting laugh. "I have no heart," he says.

"Then maybe I'm not as bad a shot as I thought."

He sighs and swallows three pills from the bedside table.

She says, "I never understood what kept stopping you. And whatever it was, where did it go?"

He never answers.

"Tell me why," she says when she knows he's asleep.

She watches him and thinks about Audrey, crashing her Cessna into a stand of trees, practicing "touch and goes," a simple exercise to renew her pilot's license which she should have been able to perform in her sleep. No mechanical problems turned up with the plane. Just one of those things that happen. Not everything has a hidden meaning.

Drew always said it wasn't really a marriage, but Jane used to question that, to herself of course. If he was Mr. Duncan and she was Mrs. Duncan, what else does it take? She knows they slept a long way apart, but she also knows suddenly that Audrey was the barrier, the thing that always stopped him, because she is the only thing that has now been removed. And because he'd been talking about shooting himself for years, but didn't until she was gone. She watches him sleep and wonders which is worse. If Drew has no heart, or if he gave it to someone else.

She rolls against him and puts her head on his shoulder, jarring him half awake.

He says, "You used to say I was the only man you

ever loved." Then he fades out again.

She did used to say that. Because at the time it was true. She rises and dresses, slips down to the lobby, and calls Steven at work. She says she loves him, and can't wait to get home. She doesn't tell him that he is the Audrey-sized barrier that stopped the momentum this time, even though it's true, and seems like wondrous news.

When they cross the border she lies again, and says she is a Canadian citizen. But it feels true, because Canada is her home now. She no longer remembers why she wanted to cross back into The States.

They stop for gas on the QEW outside Niagara Falls. They buy packaged sandwiches and sodas and put it all on his credit card.

Just as they get back to the car, he grabs her, and leans her up against the passenger door in an extended bear hug. The car is cold against her back. The air is cold around them. Over his shoulder, she sees a blow-up Santa Claus on the roof of the pump island, tied down with guy wires. She watches it sway in the frigid wind, listens to the thup-thup of it, rocking over the scene. She wonders how many days it is until Christmas, if there's still time to buy something really nice for Steven.

"I'm sorry I hurt you," he says. "Can you accept that?"

She nods, knowing he can feel it against his shoulder. Tears start, which he might feel in time. She's cold, and wants to get into the car and go home. "Don't forget your promise."

"What promise?"

"To come say goodbye." He never promised, she knows that, but she wants him to now. "If it's possible to do it."

"Will if I can."

"Promise?"

"Yes. Promise." It always takes a few tries to pin him. "I love you," he says.

She pushes him away and gets in. He comes around to the driver's side and starts the engine.

"What, Jane? What did I say wrong?"

"Remember when you threw that boarder out for not taking care of his horse? I said, 'He loves that horse.' You said, 'Bullshit. When you love a horse, you take care of him.'"

He nods, and turns on the wipers against a fresh fall of snow. "Horses are easier," he says.

Less than a month later, Drew proves that he actually does have a heart. Because the round explodes, as it is designed to, and shatters it.

She hears this four days after the fact. The funeral is over, so Jane need not agonize over whether to go. It's a great relief. The whole thing, not just the issue of the funeral. Now she knows it's really over. She decides not to say that to anyone. It would sound cold, and she doesn't mean it to.

Then she changes her mind, calls an emergency session with Bobbi, and tells her just that. Bobbi says it's a human thing to feel, and she should forgive herself for it whenever possible.

After the session she drives by Drew's farm, and opens the barn door to see if dogs wag around her legs. When they don't, she drives on to his neighbor, whose name she does not remember. She knocks on his door, and he answers, but the dogs are not wagging around as she expects.

"I wondered if Drew's dogs were okay."

"I took them to the pound," he says. "The pups'll get homes. Last stop for the old dog, as it should be."

"Okay, thanks."

She drives forty kilometers to the pound.

Mister, she is told, was humanely put down, almost as he came through the door. The Border Collies are available for adoption. She writes a check and loads them into the back of her truck.

She bathes them both before nightfall and lets them sleep in the bedroom, curled together with their chins on each other's backs. She half expects Steven to object, but he doesn't mention it. She lies in bed and listens to the comfortable sound of their breathing.

She realizes that Drew did not come to say goodbye.

She could say it only proves that isn't possible, and so delude herself, but chooses not to. She could be a step more honest and say that seeing Audrey, or even Candle, was a higher priority. But she chooses to be even more honest than that. She admits to herself that Drew never kept his promises worth a damn anyway.

In the morning she'll admit that to Bobbi. Bobbi will probably say, Okay. Now we might actually be getting somewhere.

DISAPPEARANCES

Leo Burnicke was driving home on Christmas morning when the incident took place. He had just spent three hours with his ex-wife and her new fiancé, because Lana deemed these things important for the sake of the kids, who were hardly kids after all. That and because a "no" answer would have inevitably led to discussions filled with the truth.

He was driving down the old Cotter road, making a beeline for the incident, though he didn't know it just yet. Not a soul shared the road with him. It was, after all, Christmas morning. People were home with their families. Not that the old Cotter road was clogged with people at other times of the year. He had just crested the hill when he saw the lights flash at the railroad crossing, the striped red-and-white wooden gates descend. A freight train approached the crossing, a distressingly long freight train.

"Shit," he said out loud. Somehow getting back to his own home had become an issue, a thing stuck in his brain, a destination compelling beyond all reason. "Shit," he said again.

Then he speeded up in an attempt to hit the train broadside. This was the moment that, in retrospect, Leo examined for some evidence of a decision. He felt there must have been a decision in there somewhere. It was a true enough event, a thing which came to exist, to pass, but which did not seem to originate with a thought or an idea. As it made even less sense without one, Leo was careful to add one in after the fact. In years to come he would refer to the incident as, "The day I decided to slam my pickup broadside into a train." If indeed he referred to it at all.

At first he just careened down the hill, the train a remote object, a string of boxcars in the distance, rust red and sickly green, hardly real at all. Almost theoretical. But then the pickup was doing over eighty, the compression of the tired old engine roaring in his ears, and the train was nearer, filling up his windshield, his landscape, a strange sight to be the last sight a man will ever see. By then the truck was accomplishing an even greater speed, probably over ninety, though he couldn't take his eyes off the train to look, and the combination of the engine noise and the train noise nearly deafened him. It would have driven all the thoughts out of his head anyway, even if he'd had a valid batch at the outset.

He cued himself to close his eyes, but he couldn't. He couldn't. He had to see.

A sharp crack, and the red-and-white wooden gate shattered; shards and slivers of it clattered against his windshield, bounced noisily over the roof of the truck. Then a flash of sudden blue sky. The whump of his tires over the tracks at better than ninety, the sound and impact of which he mistook for the sound and impact of dying. He found himself clear of the tracks, slamming on the brakes, skidding, tires squealing, determined not to go one foot farther until he grasped what had just transpired. He turned his head to see. Behind him, the caboose of the train lumbered off into the distance, rocking from side to side on the tracks, the way trains do.

He sat quietly for a moment, slowly arriving at the only possible logical explanation. The train had gone by. There was no other way it could have been. There was no other story to tell himself, or anyone else. Between the moment he broke the wooden gate and the moment he hit the track, the train had simply passed.

He sat a moment longer. His hands shook on the steering wheel. His thighs shook on the seat, a deep tremble that seemed to come out of the bone itself. He looked down. It humiliated him to see that he had wet himself, if only a little bit. He looked up to see a shard from the wooden gate sitting on his windshield wiper.

He accelerated and drove toward home, assuming it would dislodge and fall off. It never did. He had to pull over to take it off by hand, first checking carefully to assure himself that no one would observe. After all, there was the issue with the front of his light blue jeans. He saw no one. People were home with their families. His legs felt rubbery and weak when he walked around to remove it. They held his weight, but not by a comfortable margin.

Upon arriving home he found a good deal more of the red and white shards in the bed of his pickup, and discarded them one by one.

At the Halfway Tavern, where Leo often stopped for a beer, there was a girl. Pam was her name. Leo danced with Pam often, fast and slow songs, sometimes three times a week, but she never let him take her home, and Leo suspected she never would. In fact, he had come to hope she never would. Because they talked now. Other girls at the Halfway let him take them home. Now they did not talk to him. Lana did not talk to him. So in this case Leo was tempted to leave well enough alone.

The night after the incident, he danced with her. It was a slow number, a country-western ballad. Pam was a big, solid girl, that night in tight jeans and a pink collarless shirt. She had blond hair; Leo couldn't tell if it was natural or not. She wore it swept up, but by that time of night it was halfway down again. Tendrils of it brushed against Leo's left hand, which rested near the nape of her neck. She smelled like cigarettes, but he didn't mind that.

As he moved his legs, he thought the tremble might still be there—or maybe it was more a shadow memory of it—and he wondered if that would ever go away. Each time he laid eyes on something, he felt he had no right to, or at very least recognized how close he'd come to missing the opportunity forever.

Because he had four or five beers in him, Leo said, "What would you say if some guy told you he just out of nowhere got it in his head to slam his car into a brick wall? No reason."

He said car instead of truck so the man could not be him. He said brick wall instead of train because someone must know by now about the shattered railroad gate out on the old Cotter road.

"How could a guy who just slammed his car into a brick wall tell me anything at all?"

"Oh," Leo said. "He swerved at just the last minute."

"Then he didn't want to die."

See, that was the wrong example. He shouldn't have said brick wall. Because brick walls don't go by before you can hit them. And Leo hadn't swerved. "But still. . . for no reason."

"It wasn't for no reason," Pam said.

"Yeah, it was. He told me. No reason at all."

"Then he's lying to you."

The song ended. They stepped back and looked at one another. The tavern was quiet that night—no one else on the dance floor. Just a couple of regulars pounding them down at the bar. Pam wandered outside onto the wood porch for a smoke. Leo followed her.

"I'm pretty close with this guy," he said. "He would never lie to me."

"Then he's lying to himself," she said. She lit a cigarette. Leaned back on a porch rail. "Because nobody does anything for no reason."

He leaned on the rail, looked out into the cool night. It was maybe forty degrees that night, as cold as that neck of the woods was going to get. A sliver of crescent moon sat on top of a mountain that Leo, in his younger days, had personally climbed. He caught a blast of her smoke.

"People do things for no reason all the time."

"Bullshit," she said. She pointed at Leo with the two cigarette fingers. "People do things for reasons you can't see. Sometimes people do things for reasons *they* can't see. But nobody ever does anything for no reason. Remember that, Leo. Remember that and the world will make more sense. You won't spend so much time running around wondering what the hell is wrong with everybody."

"That would be nice," Leo said.

Leo sat in the outer office of Perry Staghorn, M.F.C.C., waiting. The furniture seemed cut for someone smaller than he. He crossed and uncrossed his legs.

At five minutes before three—his appointment time was three—the door to the inner office opened, and a shy, ashamed-looking woman scooted by, avoiding Leo's eyes. He looked up to the doorway to see a woman standing, regarding him. He wondered who she was, and when he would be invited to meet Perry Staghorn, M.F.C.C. He looked at her, waiting. She looked at him; he wasn't sure what else she might be doing. She had naturally curly hair. She wore a red suit with a straight skirt. She was younger than Leo. So many people were these days.

She said, "You must be Leo Burnicke."

"Yes," he said, as if that explained nothing.

"Then you're my three o'clock," she said. "Come in."

He didn't. He didn't get up. He didn't say anything for an embarrassing span of time.

Then he said, "You're a woman."

"Yes," she said, "I know."

"I didn't think you were a woman. That's an unusual name. For a woman."

"Perry? It's a pretty unisex name."

"I guess I thought women spelled it with an i on the end. Or an ie. Or something."

The look on her face changed. It evolved, actually. As if there were a joke in the room, a joke neither one of them got, only she was beginning to. "I spell it with a y," she said. "You heard my voice on my answering machine. And on yours. When I called you back."

"I thought that was your secretary."

"I don't have a secretary."

"Really? I would think you would."

She shifted slightly, evening her stance, and Leo heard the light sound of her nylons brushing together. "Are you uncomfortable seeing a woman? Because, if you are. . ."

"No," he said. A bit too strenuously, in fact. "No. So long as you can help me. Man, woman. Makes no difference to me."

"You seem uneasy."

"I guess I'm just uneasy with seeing any. . ." Now what, Leo? How to say it. Shrink? No. Possibly insulting. Psychiatrist? She probably wasn't one. Was an M.F.C.C. a psychiatrist? What the hell was an M.F.C.C., anyway? ". . . mental health professional."

"Right," Perry said. "I get that."

They regarded each other a moment longer. Then Leo realized it was time for him to stand up.

"Really," he said, following her into the inner office, where the furniture was no roomier, "I'm surprised. I would think someone in your position would have a secretary."

"I think we need to talk about Christmas morning, then," she said.

"No," Leo said. He was having trouble with his legs again. Crossing. Uncrossing. Neither felt right, yet he was so sure each would be an improvement, until he got there. "See? I knew you would say that. But that's not what it's about."

"Okay," she said. "Good. I'm glad you know what it's about." She waited. He crossed his legs again. "What's it about?"

"I have no idea. That's why I'm here to see you. I was hoping you would tell me."

"If you don't know what it's about," she said, "then why are you so sure it wasn't about Christmas morning?"

"Because it just wasn't. You're making me talk around in circles on purpose."

"We don't have to do this all at once. We can go at your comfort level."

I haven't even seen my comfort level around recently, Leo thought. "I'll talk about Christmas morning. Fine. I don't care. I'll talk about it all you want. I'll talk about anything you want. The reason I think it's not about that is because I'm really over her. My ex. I'm just completely over her. It's just. . .over."

"What about your kids? It's never over with your kids."

"I still see them, though. I mean, I still see the kids."

"But didn't you say that this was your last chance to see them before they move?"

"Just down to Dixon, though. I mean, couple hours' drive. After they get married. I'll have to drive farther to see the kids. They're not even kids now. The youngest is fifteen. Not really kids. Not so much. Not anymore."

A long silence. Perhaps she was waiting for him to say more.

"How does it feel to you," she said, "knowing another man will be raising your kids?"

He went to cross his legs, discovered they were crossed already, and uncrossed them instead. "They're mostly raised as it is."

"Most men would be bothered by watching their kids with a new dad."

"He's not their dad."

"No, and he never will be. But I still wouldn't blame you if the whole thing made you feel a little impotent."

"I do not have that problem," Leo said. "I got problems. But not in that department."

"I didn't mean it literally."

"How did you mean it?"

"Impotent. It means. . . powerless."

She waited. He crossed his legs again, unaware that he had ever uncrossed them. She did the same. He wondered if she had picked it up from him.

Leo said, "I was under the impression that this first session was more of just a get-to-know-each-other introductory kind of a thing."

At the end of the session she said, "I'm afraid our time is up. Shall we go ahead and schedule another appointment?"

"Let me mull it over and get back to you," he said.

A week later, Jasper called him up out of the blue, at about seven on a Saturday morning. Jasper rose with the sun, work day or no, and he harbored no guilt about waking others. "If you weren't awake," he would often say, "you should have been."

"Leo," Jasper said.

"Jasper," Leo said.

"How about I hook up the old boat trailer to the old Dodge and we'll take her down to the ocean?"

Leo sat up in bed, blinking, pretending to already be awake. "You're offering to take me fishing? Why?"

"I'm your brother," Jasper said.

"You've always been my brother. This taking me out on your boat thing is new. Why?"

A pause on the line. Then Jasper said, "You don't seem to be yourself lately."

"I'm myself."

"You don't seem to be."

"Well, I am."

"So you're saying you don't want to go fishing?"

"Jasper, you idiot, who the hell you think you called? I always want to go fishing. I just want to know why all of a sudden."

"I'm your brother."

"Yeah," Leo said. "We're clear on that."

Jasper motored them out into a kelp bed and cut the engine. The silence felt good on Leo's ears. The motion of the swells soothed him as they assembled their rods and tied off. Leo found himself needing the soothing. Jasper had this Shimano spin-casting rod, probably too light for saltwater use, paired with one of those three hundred dollar reels. How could anybody spend three hundred dollars on a reel? Why? What does it do? It takes up the extra line between you and the fish, so he comes back to the boat. If Leo's rod and reel—forty-four dollars from the hardware store—could do that, could Jasper's do it three hundred dollars' worth better? Things like that were God's way of telling you you're making too much money.

On that thought, Leo took a beer out of his cooler and popped the top. He offered one to Jasper, who shook his head. Never hurts to ask, anyway. Leo downed most of his in two swallows and then tied a three-way swivel on his line. To that he tied a lighter piece of line, only eight-pound test, and to the end of that he tied a used spark plug, one of many he kept in his bright blue tackle box. He dug around for a couple of size 2/0 hooks, then looked up to see Jasper eyeing him suspiciously.

"That's an old spark plug," Jasper said.

"Yes it is."

"Why are you using an old spark plug as a sinker?"

"Because it's free," Leo said. "Because if you fish these waters like you say you do, you know the kelp snags. So you use a free sinker and tie it on with a lighter test. Then if you have to break the line to get free of a snag, all you lose is an old spark plug. Not your hooks and not your bait. Not a fish if you got one on there."

"But then you're leaving old spark plugs strewn around on the bottom of the ocean. That doesn't seem very environmental."

"Environmental? *Environmental*?" Leo felt like reaching for another beer, but he knew Jasper was keeping track. Besides, he'd only brought a six pack. He had to pace himself. "As opposed to that?" He pointed to Jasper's two-ounce, sixty-cent pyramid sinker. "That thing is lead. Lead, as in lead poisoning. At the bottom of the ocean. How environmental is that?"

Jasper stared down at the pyramid sinker as though waiting to be introduced, and for quite a long time at that. "Well," he said, "at least it looks a little better sitting down there than a crappy old spark plug."

"So your theory is, then, that the fish don't mind being poisoned much, but they hate an unsightly mess."

"Just tie off and fish, Leo."

"This is why we don't do this more often," Leo said. "In case you were going to ask me that before the day is out."

The wind came up good and hard by early afternoon, and it whistled in Leo's ears. It rippled the surface of the ocean, and flipped over bits of kelp floating high on the water.

Jasper had been fishing with a cast-and-retrieve,

because he had to use his seven-dollar-apiece swim bait, with the painted-on eyes and everything. For that kind of money, you make the suckers swim. Leo had been using a more serviceable three-hook rig baited with squid, more or less straight down into the kelp. He used the heads, because he'd had good luck with the tentacles getting the fish's attention. The tubes he cut up and threw into the water as chum. He had two legal sand bass and a little calico rockfish to show for it. Jasper hadn't so much as fetched his stringer from his overly organized tackle box.

Then out of nowhere Jasper said, "We all know the pressure you're under."

"First off, who's 'we all'?"

"Well, me and Lorraine. Momma and Daddy. Josh. I mean, with Lana getting remarried and all, and moving away with the kids."

"Only just to Dixon."

"That's not the point, though, Leo. The point is, you being still so damned. . ."

"So damned what?"

"Obsessed with her."

"Obsessed? *Obsessed*?" Leo heard himself shouting, but it sounded far away. "Why the hell would you say that? I am so over her."

"She's all you talk about."

"I never talk about her."

"You talk about the guy she's marrying and everything you don't like about him, and you resent how much money he makes, and how he—"

"That is not the same thing."

"Hell it isn't. Leo, you—" He stopped suddenly, and

Leo knew Jasper felt something on his line. The world grew quiet, all except for the wind. Jasper whispered to himself. "Wait for it. . . Wait for it. . ." Then Jasper yanked the rod to set the hook. He fought his catch for a time, the Shimano rod bent nearly in half. Leo figured it would snap before he could land anything even halfway impressive, but a moment later Jasper put on a stiff leather glove and gaffed the fish by hand, his gloved fingers hooked deep into its gill rakers, hoisting it onto the floor of the boat. It lay still, as fish often will for a time. A beauty of a ling cod, probably long enough to be legal.

Both men scrambled for their measuring tapes at once. Leo won the race, running a tape from the nose of the fish back to its tail, a perfect twenty-four inches. The exact length required for a ling cod to be legal. Twenty-four inches exactly.

"You got it!" Leo cried. "It's a keeper."

He pulled a beer from his ice chest in wild celebration, though truthfully he felt a burn of envy. His three little fish, the biggest at thirteen inches, flapped weakly on their stringer, suddenly pathetic.

When he looked up, Jasper was holding the ling cod by the gill rakers again, dangling it over the side of the boat, its wet, mottled sides shining. Leo choked on a swallow of beer and coughed, his hands up in a desperate plea for no action, for nothing to happen, until he could speak again. "What are you doing? What in God's name are you doing?"

"It's not legal," Jasper said. "You measured it wrong. You don't run the tape over the body of the fish like that. If you do, the thickness of the fish will make it appear to measure out longer. The correct measurement is on a flat surface, between a mark you make at the point of its nose and the tip of its tail. The shortest distance between two points is a straight line."

Leo stared at the ling cod, still dangling over the water, as if the sheer force of his stare could hold the fish aloft. He'd never seen something so big and beautiful released. It made him dizzy to think he might not prevent it. The hook was still in place in the ling cod's upper lip. Jasper had cut the line close to the hook. On this point—and seemingly on this point only—the brothers agreed. It's best to leave the hook in a fish you're going to release. It'll rust away in a few days, causing much less damage than trying to haul that barb out backward through living flesh. Only, in this case, it meant letting go of a seven-dollar swim bait. Leo could see most of it; it was olive colored, with flashing hand-painted white eyes. It looked panicked. The ling cod looked relatively calm. Leo could see the stunning greenish-blue of its belly.

"Nobody measures a fish like that. Except a damn D.F.G. warden."

"Exactly. Just the guy who'll write the citation if I get caught with this."

"He won't be there. He won't. They're never there. Guys take fish like that all the time."

"Can't take the chance," Jasper said, and Leo knew he had hit the brick wall of Jasper's exactitude.

"Let me have him, then. I'll risk the fine."

Jasper shook his head. "Rules are rules for a reason," he said.

The ling cod disappeared. Looking back, Leo could

swear he never saw it fall from Jasper's gloved hand. It just evaporated. Leo lurched his upper body over the side, rocking the boat dangerously, in case he could see it go. But it was all over by then.

"That is the most heartbreaking thing I have ever seen."

"Nonsense," Jasper said.

"I mean it. Absolutely heartbreaking."

They fished for another hour. Every few minutes, the image of the disappearing ling cod wedged its way back into Leo's mind. Each time, he felt a sharp sense of loss in his belly, an absolute inability to comprehend how something so big and beautiful, so rare and sought after, could be gone. He kept it to himself, pretty sure Jasper would not understand.

Neither caught another thing.

As they landed the boat on the beach, Leo said, "It just broke my heart to watch that fish go."

Jasper lost his temper then, and raised his voice. "Oh my God, Leo, are you still obsessing about that? See, that's the problem with you. You just can't let go of anything. It's just never over for you. It was a fucking fish, Leo. Fish are not heartbreaking. Families are heartbreaking. You don't lose your heart in a fishing incident. Get things in perspective." Then he clearly felt guilty for yelling, and tried to make it up to Leo. "Forget it," he said, as if everybody else let go just that easily. "We'll stop by the house, and Lorraine will clean your fish."

Leo glanced briefly at Jasper's ever-present gold

wedding band. "I don't need Lorraine to clean my fish. Why should she?"

"We're all family."

"I can clean a goddamn fish," Leo said, raising his voice a bit now himself.

"Fine. Suit yourself," Jasper said, and waddled up the launch ramp to go fetch the truck.

Later, at home, for the first time ever, Leo cut himself on his filet knife. He had cut off the head of the little calico rockfish, snapping its spine just behind the gills with his big kitchen shears. He used a bloody fishing towel to hold the headless fish steady in the sink, and—starting at the vent—slit its underbelly with the filet knife and scooped the guts out onto a piece of old newspaper.

Then he stopped to clean the sink a little with his hands, brushing blood and scales into the catch-all in the drain. While he did this, he thought how this was one great thing about not living with a woman— cleaning a fish right in your kitchen sink. He thought about the ling cod again, disappearing from Jasper's gloved hand—thought how many great dinners it would have made, if Jasper had let him have it. Or, better yet, it he'd caught it himself. On that thought he caught the pad of his little finger on the razor-sharp tip of the filet knife, which was still in the sink, half-covered by the bloody towel. He caught it in a downward sweep that sent it biting into the flesh until bone stopped it. Then he had to reverse the motion to unskewer himself again.

He wrapped his finger in a paper towel to stanch the bleeding, bent over himself as if ashamed. Indeed, he was ashamed. You pay attention around knives, and you don't cut yourself. That was just the rule. For one strange, sudden moment it almost made him cry, or at least want to, but he put the sensation away again.

He removed the paper towel and checked the wound to see if it required a stitch or two, but it was a puncture, not a slice. A deep puncture. He wondered it he could even get the bleeding stopped in time to finish cleaning and cooking his dinner.

Maybe it was no big deal. He couldn't decide. On the one hand, he knew better than to let his attention lapse around a filet knife. On the other hand, it was a pretty small injury to stress about, particularly for a man who had recently attempted to broadside a train.

A few minutes later he wrapped it tightly with a Band-Aid. It continued to bleed, but he paid it little attention.

Too well fed on six fried fish filets with potatoes, Leo fell asleep in his lumpy overstuffed chair. When he woke again it was dark, and he'd left no lights on in the house. His little finger throbbed painfully, and his back ached from sleeping in a bad position. He turned on the light and pulled off the Band-Aid. His finger was coated with dried blood and deeply bruised, as if most of the bleeding had taken place under the skin.

He sat a moment trying to decide if he'd been dreaming about that ling cod, or if it was simply the initial thought to greet him upon waking.

He found himself seized with a desire to call his daughter. He squinted at the clock, saw it was after midnight. Lana would filet and deep-fry *him* if he called this late. So he sat and ached about that for a time. Then he decided it wouldn't have helped anyway. It really wasn't his fifteen-year-old daughter he wanted to talk to, it was his little girl, and he hadn't seen her for quite some years.

"I must say I was surprised," Perry Staghorn said. "Very surprised that you called. I didn't expect you ever would. I didn't quite get the part of your message about the fish."

"What I asked was," Leo said, pleased at the calm tone of his voice, "what do you make of a guy who gets his heart broke over the loss of a fish he didn't even catch, but who can't seem to care less that his own family is disappearing?"

"I don't think that's your case," Perry said. "After all, you did try to run into a train."

"Oh." Then, after a long silence, "I guess I see your point about that. Let me ask you another question, then. Do you think I have some special purpose in life? Because I tried real hard to hit that train. I was staring right at that caboose when I hit the track. If it hadn't been the caboose, I wouldn't be sitting here. But I am. You think it's for a reason, like there's some important thing I haven't done yet? Do you believe that way about life?"

"I think the more important question," she said, "is what *you* believe about life."

Leo grunted and rocked back in his too-small chair. "See, this is what I hate about. . . mental health professionals. No offense. But you're always saying things like, How do *you* feel about it? Or, What do *you* think it means?"

"Yeah, point taken, but, really, Leo. . . are you really spending eighty-five dollars an hour to find out more about how I see the world? Isn't it really more about what you think about it?"

"What I think about the world," Leo repeated.

"Right. What do you think about the world?"

Leo sat still a moment. Uncharacteristically still. He did not cross or uncross his legs, or wish to. He felt the stillness in his body as something new. He turned his inner eye to the question at hand. Minutes seemed to pass, though in truth they may only have been seconds.

"I think I'm in no way cut out for it," he said at last.

For reasons he would not understand for months to come, she took that as a good sign from him, and said it would do for a start.

FIVE SINGING GARDENERS AND ONE DEAD STRANGER

If you were poor, you could buy a used fax machine off a dead guy and not take any crap from anybody as a result. And you are poor; that's the unfair thing. But your fiancé is not. So you have to take the crap on his behalf, with your own name written in, where it seems not to fit.

But you do it anyway, don't you? Just to prove all that stubbornness won't marry out of you.

When you bring it home to palatial Montecito, notice there are five gardeners at work on your grounds. Five. Well, your fiancé's grounds. Call them yours, why don't you? You'll learn to, sooner or later.

You don't speak enough Spanish to ascertain why five, but assume your fiancé complained that the grounds look seedy. He did say that. And you said, yeah, I see what you mean. But without his eyes to see through, it might have looked like a palace to you. Not even a seedy one.

When you get inside with your second-hand thermal fax, step into the front closet and punch numbers into the alarm system before it calls the police and has you arrested as an intruder. So far as you know, this contributes nothing to the sense that you don't exactly belong here.

Take your new purchase into your new office and send a fax to Alan. Why Alan? Why indeed. Most everyone you know could receive a fax, and answer this simple question: Did you receive it? But don't ask any of them. Only Alan.

A few minutes later, receive a fax back. The first words you've heard, loosely speaking, from Alan in about seven weeks. Well, not about seven. Seven. Exactly. It only seems longer.

It says: What's Wrigley Michigan? Is that a business name? It sounds like a small town in the Great Lakes region.

Pick up the handset and call him at home, even though you never had the nerve to before. Tell him you have no idea what he's talking about.

"Your sender I.D.," he says.

Stop and ponder a moment. Decide if you should admit you don't know what a sender I.D. is.

After awhile he'll grow tired of waiting and say, "It reads across the top of every fax. Somehow you must have programmed it in there, Suse. Think hard."

Think hard, because Alan told you to. Then say, "Maybe it's the old owner's sender I.D."

"You bought it used?"

Say, "What's wrong with that?" Then tell him to wait a minute, there's a train going by. You can't hear him. While you're both waiting, pretend he won't tell you what's wrong with that.

After you've studied the manual for half an hour, you should be able to program your own sender I.D., erasing the name Wrigley Michigan forever. You know it's not a business name because you bought the machine from the dead guy's brother, Holland Michigan. Just assume weird names run in the dead guy's family.

When you're done, fax Alan back with this question: What does it say on top now?

Wait too long for an answer, and, while you're waiting, try to stop doing that thing you keep doing, where you hope this takes all day. Where you hope he comes over and shows you, because it's something you just can't work out on the phone.

Don't jump when the fax rings again. Try not to, anyway.

Read the following on the curling paper: It says Susan Lindeman, with the wrong time. Time. This is harder than you thought it would be. Watch, too intensely, the paper feed until you see there's more. Try not to be disappointed when it's only this: What did Wrigley Michigan turn out to be?

Call him at home. Say, "The guy's name."

"Why would Wrigley Michigan sell his fax machine? Unless he was having problems with it." Try to answer fast, before he can say, "You did buy a plain paper fax. Right? Don't tell me Wrigley was moving up to plain paper and you bought his old thermal. My God, Suse, what's the point of marrying a rich guy if you won't spend any of his money?"

It's what you get for not answering fast enough.

Try saying this: "Wrigley Michigan sold his fax machine because he's dead." See what a good answer that turned out to be? All that other stuff just disappeared.

"You bought a dead guy's fax? What did he die from?"

Tell the truth. Say, "I didn't ask."

"Weren't you even curious?"

Lie. Say, "Why would I be interested in a dead stranger?"

"Well. I'd want to know if his soul is resting in peace. Maybe it's haunted."

"A haunted fax machine?"

"Sure. Why not?"

Tell him you liked ghost stories better in the old-fashioned low-tech days.

Try not to be hurt when he manufactures no excuse to prolong the conversation.

Before tackling the onerous task of an outgoing message, step outside to breathe. Smile at the gardeners. All five of them. Even though it seems to make them nervous. Pretend not to know they were happier with you inside.

You are the only person you know who learned to say, "*Lo siento para mi Español*," in order to apologize for your Spanish, which *es no muy bueno*. Nobody else in Montecito says this. As far as you know. Actually it's a damn safe bet. That's why you say it. *Lo siento.*

Because nobody else will. Because you want them to know you're closer to being one of Them than one of Us. You want them to know you don't exactly belong here, either. So now they know. But they're still happier with you inside.

You are The Señora, poor fit or no.

Go back inside.

Call Alan at home, for the third time in one day. Even though in the four years prior to this you never did, not even once. Ask him to call on your fax line and leave a message.

Then try desperately but unsuccessfully to figure out how to monitor messages.

After he's hung up the phone, succeed in playing the whole thing back. Hear this: "Listen. Susan. Do this thing or don't, but be happy with what you decide. You're not even married yet, and already you're trying to divorce yourself from the whole scene. I mean, come on, Suse. He would have let you use his fax. If you wanted your own, he would have bought you a brand new one. Plain paper. I'm only saying all this because I care. I'm going to hang up now. Forget you ever knew me."

Now listen to it three times more. Because it's Alan's voice and you might not hear it again. Think about calling him back. But don't. Whatever you do, don't. Because you've scraped by three times now, and your luck might run out. Next time she might answer.

Consider pocketing the microcassette and buying a new one. So you never have to tape over this. While you're deciding, more messages will play. Lots more. But not for you, of course. For Wrigley Michigan.

Listen anyway.

A whole tape full. Discover, to your surprise, how much you can learn about a dead stranger by listening to twenty-six of his phone messages.

When you're done listening, sit marveling over how much of Wrigley Michigan's life you now possess. Except that Wrigley Michigan has no life. But maybe he still could, if you possessed it for him.

Now scratch that thought. That was a stupid thought.

Rewind the tape and play it again. Fast forward through the calls from his wife, because they're boring. Fast forward through the three from the pharmacy, asking why he hasn't come in to pick up his photos. Maybe later you should stick your head into the pharmacy and tell them why not. They couldn't think ill of Wrigley if they knew why not. It's such a good excuse.

When you get to the cluster of calls from his lover, Anne, start your good cry. Then rewind and listen to the Anne calls again, because you weren't quite finished. Notice how she calls him Rig, and how that makes you uncomfortable and sad. First try to pin down why. Later try not to. In neither endeavor will you enjoy complete success.

When the tape plays out and stops, listen. The gardeners are singing. All five, from the sound of it. In Spanish.

In harmony. Not a rehearsed-sounding thing. One of them just starts, and then the others add their voices. You know it's a Mexican song, even though you can't understand the words. It's definitely not Montecito they're singing about.

This is the moment it will hit you. Somewhere south of your head. Your head is still woefully ignorant, but your gut gets the message all of a sudden. They brought this song here because it's something from home. Because this is a foreign land.

Look out the window. You'll see they're right.

Walk out with just the clothes on your back, though you have no intention of returning. Put on your sunglasses so they won't know you've been crying.

As you come down the path, your presence will still their voices. Tell them, "*Lo siento*."

Drive away fast so they can get back to singing.

Since you have no special plans, drive into the upper village and pick up Wrigley Michigan's photos, because it's been twenty-eight days already, and after thirty days, they have threatened, they will throw them away.

Tell them you misplaced the stub. Tell them you're a friend of Wrigley's, even though it's clear they don't care who you are.

Tell yourself you do this out of idle curiosity, though you know it's something more important. Something about too much of Wrigley having been discarded already.

Sit in the car and flip through them. Notice how it hurts that Wrigley is not much older than you. How big and dark his eyes are. How easily he could be a friend of yours if he wasn't a stranger. Notice how you can tell that's Anne, because you know how he feels about Anne. Because he doesn't look bored.

Try to forget the ultimatum she issued him shortly before he died. How she told him to decide what mattered.

Pretend you don't know that Wrigley died about this. Think instead that he just had an accident in his car or something. Remember to pretend that dying in an accident is not the same thing as dying on purpose. Think how sad he was at the end and pretend you have no idea how that might feel.

Now pretend you're not going to go see Alan. No, never mind. Don't bother with that last one. You've wasted enough time as it is.

Cruise by his house and do the three short beeps on your car horn, and then wait around the corner like you always did. Even though her car is not there. Do it just to be safe.

While you're waiting, look at the pictures again. This time notice how pretty Anne is, and understand why he needed her. Try. It shouldn't be hard.

When Alan gets into the passenger seat, don't look him in the eye. Don't tell him why you're here. Whatever you do, don't suggest you go out to his studio in Carpinteria.

You won't take your car for the ten minute drive to

Alan's studio. You won't take his car. You'll go by freight train.

Sit in the heavy gray gravel by the side of the tracks, not half a mile from the spot where they cross in front of your beachfront home. Your fiancé's beachfront home. Your former fiancé. Listen to the sound that comes off the tracks when the train is only half a mile away, and wonder if the noise of the train is, at this moment, drowning out the singing gardeners. Just for a split second you're allowed to wish you were there.

Notice how many of the big rusted spikes have come loose, lying scattered in the gravel. How trains barrel along this track even as it comes undone. Pretend this is not a metaphor, or, if it is, that you don't know for what.

When it turns out to be a passenger train, a sleek silver Amtrak, ask Alan, "Why are we doing this again?" Shout to be heard. When the train has roared away to the south, ask again, because he didn't hear you.

"Because you want this."

"Oh." You didn't know you wanted this, but he knew, and that's some comfort to you now.

When the next train is a Southern Pacific freight, and it's clear you will be compelled to jump it, ask, "Why do I want this again?" Ask fast; in a minute you won't be able to hear each other. The train will drown out everything except that little jangle of fear.

"Because the part of you that would jump a freight train has been getting lost lately."

Ask yourself if you even knew there was part of you that would jump a freight train. This will help you pretend you don't understand what he means.

Miss on the first jump. Land on your feet if possible. Look up to see that Alan made it. That he's dangling comfortably from the side of a boxcar, holding the ladder, his feet planted firmly on it, reaching one hand down to you. Realize that if you don't try again, he'll ride off without you.

Run to keep up. Try to shake that familiar feeling.

When he grabs you, when you grab him, you're going to feel like you're falling. Think, So what's new? Know that you probably are falling. Teeter there, take a good hold, stand with your feet on a rung and smile. Know that you didn't leave home for nothing. As you rattle along the Carpinteria bluffs, notice how the ocean spreads out forever. How the oil platforms stain the horizon. Feel Alan's arm around your waist. Pretend it's only there as a safety precaution, and that you're not going to his studio for any special reason.

When it's time to bail, consider for a minute riding the train until it stops, to avoid jumping. Look down at the rushing gravel, the ocean palisade cliff, and wonder if you've brought enough money to get home from Southern California. Then, when Alan jumps, stop wondering.

Jump.

Land on your feet and try to stay that way. It won't work, though. Give up and pitch forward, landing hard on both knees, and the heels of your hands. You'll find it's surprisingly painful. Crouch there for a minute, appreciating that you survived. Now open your eyes.

Notice that you're close enough to the bluff to see over the edge; feel that queer sensation of almost falling. Wonder if Wrigley Michigan fell, jumped off a bridge or drove his car off a cliff, and if this feeling bonds you two together even more solidly. Okay, enough of that. Stop wondering how Wrigley died. There is no doubt that he fell.

Take the pictures out of your pocket and drop them a hundred feet into the surf.

Accept Alan's help in rising. Say, "Ouch." When he asks if you really hurt yourself, say, "No." It's not like you never lied to him before.

Walk with him the three blocks to his studio, without admitting that you've really hurt your knees.

Don't say ouch again, no matter how real the temptation.

When he rolls off you, lie still for a minute and listen to a train go by. Then get up and limp naked to the little half-sized refrigerator in the corner of his studio. Break a whole tray of ice cubes into a dish towel, then limp back and lie next to him, in case you never get to again. Hold the ice on your knees, which have begun to swell.

Assume Alan is napping until he says, "What the hell is wrong with you, Susan?"

Say, "I just banged up my knees a little," even though you know that's not what he means.

"That's not what I mean." Pretend that could be the end of the conversation. "You love him." When he says that, know it's true, though it's okay to have ambivalent feelings about being reminded.

Wonder if Wrigley Michigan loved his wife. Before you even finish wondering you'll know what a stupid question it is. Of course he did. Or there wouldn't have been a problem.

Tell Alan all about Wrigley Michigan. Tell him that Anne felt she'd waited long enough and wanted him to move one way or another. Tell him that Wrigley didn't have much time to figure out what mattered. And that's such a hard question, too: What matters? Tell Alan that Wrigley loved his wife, even though she was boring. Tell him Anne is pretty, though he could probably guess.

Throw in the singing gardeners.

When you're done, listen to the silence. Now listen to him break it. "You haven't changed much."

Say, "Thank you," though it's clearly not a compliment.

"Go home to him."

"If I don't. . .." Wait as long as possible before finishing that thought. If you must finish it at all. "Are you ever going to leave her?" Squeeze your eyes shut and try to persuade the words to slink home unnoticed. Hope he won't answer.

"If I did, I wouldn't be what you want anymore. If I did, and you could have all of me, then you'd be off fucking somebody else to hide out from me."

Start to tell him that's ridiculous, then think better of it. Instead, tell him you don't know if you can be happy there.

Here's what he will say: "The question is whether you can be happy, period."

Say you don't know yet.

He'll tell you to bloody well find out. That's how he is. He'll say if not, you can't be happy anywhere. And if so, you can be happy there.

When you get back from calling the cab, he'll say you should have forgotten him long ago.

Promise to do better this time.

Just before you leave, he'll say, "Try going back there as yourself. Stop trying so hard to fit."

Say maybe you'll just do that.

Know you'll never say anything else to him, ever, never hear him say anything else to you. Expect that to hurt. It's okay to be surprised and a little disappointed when, just for this one moment, it doesn't.

Arrive home to find that the gardeners have packed up and gone.

Go inside and erase the microcassette.

Then spend the rest of the afternoon deciding whether or not, when he gets home, you'll tell him how badly you fucked up today. Be assured that whatever you end up doing in that regard, it will be a decision made with his best interest at heart.

While you're thinking, ice your knees again. Decide that if poor individuals from a foreign land can grow accustomed to this place, so can you.

Make a mental note to do more singing.

SUBWAY DANCER AND SNAKE

Whap. The thick soles of his unlaced high-tops hit the word. Then the concrete floor. It's on the wall of the station, the ugly tile wall. The word. Whap. He hits it again.

It takes a good running start to do that. It takes juice to do it. Steam. And he has that, all right. But it also takes balance, which is harder.

Whap. The word DICK scrawled on the wall in something like greasy pencil. Greasy and ugly, like the word, like the thing really is. Ugly. Whap. Then his legs pull back under him, to land on his feet.

Three boys come down the stairs into the long tube of subway. Down the tube, that's where he is. Every night of his life, where he is. Down the tube. Big boys, not like him. Grown-on-the-outside boys. Hurt-you boys. So he goes into Crazydance. Crazydance works every time.

Spinning, spinning. A dizzying spin, with a long karate kick on every revolution, and a shout, no words, just a sound, a crazy sound. Round and round in front of them, burning off that crazy sound. Nobody likes crazy. Even mean boys don't like crazy. Crazy is the unknown. The might-not-be-scared. Might not roll over just right. The boys roll their eyes and pass.

The roar of the train. He stands panting, watching their backs. Watching the opposite side of the platform flash through the windows of the train, slowing. Slowing. Doors open. Boys board.

Crazydance. It works every time.

Doors close. He shouts one of his favorite things. One of those good things to say. "Kids, don't try this at home." If he shouts it, and it's one of those good things to say, it always comes right out. Never gets stuck. Never. Kids, don't try this at home. Even Crazydance won't work at home. Nothing will save you from the ones you love. "Run for your life." Another good thing to say.

The train pulls out. He shouts another real thing, a plain, uncrazy thing. "I can do this." That's the best one, when it feels true.

He turns back to his work. Runs at the word. Jumps at it, aims at it, flies at it. His sneakers heading right for it. But it's wrong. Like he took off too soon. Like he let those boys fuck with his timing. Like there's one more stair, and you thought no more stairs, so you fall. His legs snap out straight, and the wall's not there yet. He falls. Feels his long hair swipe around. No control. Lost control. Out of control. His head smacks hard on the concrete. Hard. He lies still.

Bad night. No control tonight. No juice. He blinks, and the world feels weird. Gray and half lost. Then it goes nearly normal again. He sits up and touches the back of his own head. His fingers come away bloody.

I hurt myself.

J hurt himself.

He stands up to wait for the next train. Just like anybody waits for a train. Still, and looking down the dark tube. His jeans jacket laps down over his fingers, like it should. Clothes should hide you, cover you like a blanket, like darkness. He feels dizzy and a little strange.

Sitting duck.

J is a sitting duck.

He will ride all night as always, but will not be safe. Maybe better off at home. No. Never be. He touches the blood on the back of his hair and waits for the train.

J is sleepy. The worst thing in the world to be. Lights flashing in the long tube, rattle of the car to rock him, and his head sinks back. He's sitting on a seat back, to be tall. And his head rolls back, touches the window, and the pain wakes him. J hurt himself.

There's a boy sitting near him, too near, really. Empty goddamn car, go sit over there. A soft-faced black boy maybe J's age or older, but bigger. Big but soft. Bigger than him, like everybody. Simple-looking. Maybe stupid. Boy smiles at him.

J says, "Touch me I'll kill you."

He comes awake. It's morning nearly. Light bleeding through a window. What window? He is not on the subway. He is in an apartment. Somebody's apartment.

Fortunately not his own. Head hurts bad. He is sleeping on a mattress on the floor. He has forgotten who he is, why he is, what this place is.

J is a sitting duck.

He feels an arm draped over him. He screams.

He is on his feet now, kicking at nothing and screaming and cursing. "Don't touch me nobody touches me goddamnit I'll kill you I mean it you touch me I'll fucking kill you."

The big soft boy looks up sleepy from the mattress. Too stupid to be scared.

J says, "You f—f—" He tries again, and again, but that hard F sound. He didn't shout it. He should have shouted it. Now he needs the word faggot, but it's stuck. It's too late now. It will dig in, never come. He wants to tell the big soft boy that he hates faggots. But now it will never come.

The boy says, "I use'ta stutter. My mom put me in special speech class. I still do sometimes. Not bad like before. You fell asleep on the subway. You musta hurt your head. I carried you back here."

"Why?"

"So you don't get hurt."

"Where's your mom?"

"She works nights. Don't get home 'til eight."

"I can't sleep here. You'll touch me."

"No I won't. If you don't want."

J stares into the boy's strangely, openly simple face. A trick there somewhere. "Are you stupid?"

"Well. I ain't smart."

"I'll say." He finds his way through the thin dawn light to the door. Seven locks. "Let me out of here," he says.

Boy gets up and begins to unravel the locks, starting at the top. He's a full head taller than J, like everybody. Fat and broad, like he'd be big even if he wasn't fat. He says, "Gotta name?"

"J."

"Like the bird?"

"No, like the letter."

"That ain't much of a name."

"It's just enough." It's what a name should be. Just the opposite of clothes, which should be big, like a loose envelope. But a name. "Get in, get out." Another good thing to say. His mother named him Jeremiah. Gave him that name to make it easier to catch him. Jeremiah. Your hair grows while you're saying it. Someone can touch you while you're waiting for that name to be over. His mother gave him that. J doesn't want anything his mother gave him.

The last lock comes away. "You can sleep in the place down the hall," the soft boy says.

"Where? Show me." A place to sleep? A real place.

"Coupl'a crack dealers busted off all the locks. But nobody'll go in there, because of the snake. You like snakes? You scared'a snakes?"

"You're crazy. What would a s—" He should have shouted it. It gets stuck.

"Last people moved out left a snake. Crack dealers went in to catch him. Worth money. Cost a lotta money, big snake like that. Couldn't catch him, though."

"What kinda snake?"

"I dunno."

"Rattlesnake?"

"Squeezer kind."

"I ain't afraid of that."

He walks down the hall. Away from the soft boy. Past the door of the sleeping place, left open. A crack open. A sleeping place. He could come back here tonight. Sleep here until his head is okay. He peers in the open door to see if he can see a snake.

"I ain't afraid of that," he says out loud. Quiet, but it doesn't stick. I ain't afraid of that.

But he doesn't go in.

Night again, so he goes back. Sleeps in the new place. On a folded blanket on the floor. All night. Weird and nice. Sleep all night. His head is bad. Hurts bad. He never sees a snake. But nobody touches him, and he sleeps.

And then when it's dark again comes back.

Three nights down a sound wakes him. A tiny scream. A thin little squeal for somebody's life. He opens his eyes. All his limbs, his brain, his insides, frozen. Everything stiff and still. Little light from the streetlamp, but not enough. He freezes still for his eyes to adjust. Sees a trace of movement. Sees the snake. Sees the snake has a rat. A wriggling rat. A slowing rat. A still rat. A dead rat. Wrapped around it like a knot, a big brutal fist. He can see now. The big greasy staring filthy eyes of the rat. The snake eases, lets the dead rat down onto the filthy floor. Opens its mouth wider than should even be possible. Opens its mouth wider than any mouth should ever be able to go. Starts with the rat's head.

J's limbs warm and loosen. Half the rat is inside now, the snake's head a sheath, a glove. Convulsing in waves, drawing the rat in. As the snake's head takes the hips of the rat it rises, arches up off the floor, into the beam of the streetlamp. Snake head hangs in the air in the light, the greasy tail of the rat disappearing slowly down its throat.

Then all is still. The lump moves slow, becomes part of the belly of the snake.

The snake moves. Slides around toward J and moves. J can hear it, the soft swish of snake belly on cool floor. J still, thrilled and afraid. The snake rises over the mountain of his knees. J can feel the weight of it, the waves of muscular pulse. Feel the lump of rat pass over his knees. A shiver of a different fear runs in him, a beautiful kind.

In that dim moment J sees about want. Sees wanting from the other side, how to want for something. Not always have to be the down side of somebody else's want. A sitting duck.

The tip of the snake's tail slips off him. He watches the snake slide behind the old brown refrigerator. So he knows now. Where to go to find the object of his desire again.

"You're mine," he informs the retreating snake. "I'm going to make you mine." He says it like he can. Maybe he can. Maybe this is what power feels like.

In the morning he works the old brown refrigerator out from the wall. Wiggles it out. One side at a time.

Looks behind. It's there. Yeah. It is, all right. Coiled up on the refrigerator motor. Gold eyes like gems. Tongue flicks the air. Maybe he can tame it. Teach it to coil around his arm. Coil all night on the subway. Dancing around and around with this snake coiled on his arm. Ride the train with his eyes closed, who's to stop him? Who would come close?

He reaches out to touch the snake. A quick movement from the snake's head. He pulls his hand back. Five lines of blood appear from nowhere on his knuckles. From nowhere. He couldn't feel. Something in the snake's mouth so sharp, like razors, he couldn't feel. He could have sworn the snake had no teeth. Blood wells and drops to the floor. So much blood.

How to make it stop? He wants to press something to it, but it would have to be something clean. He looks around. Nothing here is. He takes his wounded hand to the sink. He'll run water on it. But the faucet doesn't run. Maybe it will get infected. Maybe snake bites get infected. At home there are things. Not many things, but some. Iodine, which will hurt, and ointment, which maybe won't. And gauze pads. Maybe he'll have to go home.

He sticks his head behind the refrigerator again. The snake licks the air. "Okay," J says. "You don't want to be touched. I get that."

J visits a man in a pet store near his apartment. Too near, but it's day. Probably okay. He looks around, while the pet store man sells a rat. It's a reptile pet store, mostly reptile. The rat is probably not a pet.

They never call it a rat. They call it a feeder. It's white, with pink eyes. Not filthy. Not greasy. J feels bad for just a second.

Pet store guy says, "Can I help you, kid?" Like the best J could ever do is steal.

J looks around at the tanks. Komodo Dragons and big Ball Pythons and Rosy Boas. Four, five hundred dollars. His snake is a Rosy Boa. He knows that now. Four, five hundred dollars. You could buy a lot of safe with that. A lot of distant.

"What if I had a snake to sell?"

"Do you have a snake to sell?"

"I know where there is one."

"Bring it in, let me see."

"How much?"

"Depends on the snake."

"Like that one." He points to the five hundred dollar Rosy Boa. "How much?"

"If it's healthy, maybe one-fifty. I gotta see it."

"But you'll sell it for five hundred."

"I'm in the business."

J looks around at the man's business. And sees that the snakes are his prisoners. That's the man's business. To take snakes and make sure they're never free. He walks to the counter. Looks at the man. Not liking him. And the man not likes him right back.

"Only one thing, though. He doesn't like to be touched."

"They never do at first. They gotta get used to it." Looks down at J's hand. The five knuckle slashes. A little sneer. "Gotta know how to handle 'em," he says.

J goes home.

Walks up the five flights. Looks in. Listens in. Nothing moves.

He washes his hand in the sink. It stings. He doesn't yell out. That's the first thing you learn. You shut up about it, whatever it is.

Dries it on toilet paper. Bleeding again. Puts on ointment. A gauze pad. But there's no white tape. He'll have to use regular tape, from the kitchen.

Goes into the kitchen. Hears his mother come in. Laughing. Two voices. Freezes. All his insides, his brain, his limbs, cold. Still. Blood seeps through the pad.

His mother appears out of nowhere in the kitchen door. Happy. Maybe high. A man over her shoulder. Eyes flash at him, strong eyes. Maybe mean eyes. Maybe not safe. Those eyes.

"Jeremiah," his mother says. Even slower than usual. Makes it sound even longer. "Jeremiah, you have been gone. For days. I hate that. You are not pulling your weight." Everything frozen. "Starting tonight, you're back. Got it?"

He could never, never, never say no. Never.

"Yes, M—M—" She moves off down the hall with the man behind her, relieving J of his duty to finish the word.

J runs away. Runs out of the apartment, down the stairs two at a time. The gauze pad drops off. Lost forever.

He heads back to his sleeping place. His snake place. In the hall, he sees the boy. The soft boy. With his mother. Holding her hand. So he knows now, about that boy. This is more than just stupid. Thirteen, fourteen year old boy, holding his mother's hand. That's more than stupid, that's . . . something more. She looks pretty. Nice. She must be nice. The worst she does is leave him alone all night. Imagine.

The soft boy looks over his shoulder at J. When they've passed.

His mother says, "What you lookin' at?"

"That's J. I know him."

"Where you know him from?"

"Nowhere."

That word. It's so perfect. So right. He remembers, clearly. Meeting that boy nowhere.

He wants to say something. Something he never said for real. Never meant for real. But maybe that's wrong, to say that. Maybe say that, you're a sitting duck. But maybe it's okay. But by the time he thinks maybe it's okay they turn the hall corner. Gone.

He goes inside.

The snake is moving across the floor. He can't believe it. Can't believe his luck. Things this good never happen.

He moves up behind the snake and grabs it right behind the head. The snake thrashes. Whips its strong muscle of a body against J's arm. Fights. But it can't bite. Just can't. J's got it. Snake is got. J has won. Until when he lets go. Then he can be bitten.

Snake is all panic. Fighting for its life. Doesn't want to be touched. J lets go. On purpose. Pulls his hand back, fast. The snake whips away under the couch, knocking aside an old abandoned box of broken crayons. J sits beside the couch, watching his hand swell. The old wounds. No new ones. Not this time.

"I'm sorry," he says. He's never said that either. Not if he didn't have to. "I'm sorry. I'm sorry. I'm sorry."

Dusk comes, his hand swells more. Darkens. And he's still saying it. "I'm sorry."

He picks up one of the crayons. Walks out of his sleeping place for the last time, because it's not his. It belongs to the snake. Walks to the door of the soft, more-than-stupid boy and his nice mother. Very small on the door, he writes THANK YOU.

In his head he breaks into the pet store in the middle of the night. Glass door. Just kicks it in. Waits for the alarm. No alarm. Or silent alarm. Then he thinks, nobody steals snakes. Nobody that brave.

He knocks the tops off all the tanks. And leaves.

Looks back. Rounds the corner and looks back. Sees the first one slither out. It fills him with juice. Steam. So he dances back, dances down the street beside the escapee. "You don't have to get used to nothing," he shouts.

But he doesn't try to touch it. Runs the other way, for the subway. "We're free." he yells. A new good thing to say. Best one, really. We don't have to get used to nothing.

In real life there's a metal grate on the door. But still.

One is free. His is. He is.

They don't have to get used to nothing.

Then finally he goes to the free clinic for his hand. It's infected.

Receptionist asks if he's on the street. If he wants a safe place to sleep.

Yeah.

He says, yeah. He says, thank you.

REASONS FOR LOVE

"Kid?"

"Why do you love me, Lenny?"

He shook his head abruptly and kicked his feet free of the tangled blankets. He'd fallen off the bed diving for the phone.

"Kid, where are you? You need to come home so I can take care of you."

"You didn't answer my question, Lenny."

"I understand. You need reassurance—" An insignificant lie. He didn't understand how anyone could need more assurance than he'd given her, or what more he could do.

"No, you don't get it, Lenny. I know you love me. I believe you. I want to know why."

"Why?" He swallowed through a dry lump in his throat. There were dozens of reasons, hundreds maybe, but all milky and indistinct, like words you'd use to write a poem, one the reader might feel but not really understand. And his brain felt deadened by sleep. "Kid, that's a tough question."

"I have to go, Lenny."

Pain in her voice, touchingly, sickeningly familiar. He could only be angry if he didn't hear the pain.

"Kid, wait. Don't hang up. Please. When are you coming home?" He finished the question on principle, as though the dial tone might know. He stared at the receiver in his hand, then hammered it against the floor a few times. "Why do you do this, Kid? Shit. I hate this."

He looked up to see Kid's cat, blinking in the half-darkness, watching.

"Don't stare at me like that, Cruiser."

The cat trotted over and rubbed the top of her head against his cheek. He pulled her close, too close, and she vaulted away again, leaving an accidental bleeding scratch on his bare chest.

He climbed back into bed, dabbed at the scratch with a Kleenex, then, after a moment staring at the ceiling, let out a belated "Ow."

When the bell sounded the end of the period, his class shot through the door in one great, teeming lump. The lone straggler was Kevin Watts, too focused on cool to gain much speed. Lenny picked up his yardstick, the one that doubled as a blackboard pointer, and held it across the door to block Kevin's escape. The boy's eyes rimmed white with panic, a wild animal watching the herd thunder off without him. Lenny swung the door closed.

"What'd I do?"

"What's the scuttle, Kev?"

"What's the what?"

"The scuttle. The word." He sat down and put his feet on the desk, hoping to pass for unconcerned. "I make a simple announcement. I'll be gone for a while. And everybody's got whispering to do."

Kevin rolled his eyes to the ceiling, grabbed at the visor of his cap where it touched the back of his neck, and jerked it back and forth. "Oh, man. Mr. Rosen. How come I gotta be your man on the street?"

"You were the last gazelle in the herd. I'm a hungry lion. Bang, you're dead. It's called natural selection."

Kevin stared at the spot on the blackboard, just over Lenny's left shoulder. "Okay, okay. Word is, it's about your . . . you know. Girlfriend."

"My fiancée, you mean."

"Yeah. That's what I mean."

"What about her?"

"Well, just that she's kinda . . . you know. Spun."

He overrode the temptation to ask for a definition. It worked, in context. Spun. Close enough.

"So, in other words, I'm a laughing stock."

The boy's face opened and took on expression. "Aw, no, Mr. Rosen, you're like a hero. Like a stud."

"Now why would that be?"

Kevin leaned over the desk, a friendly conspiracy. "'Cause some of us actually seen her. Mack seen her, he thought she was your daughter, but I said no, he don't got a daughter, that's his . . . you know."

"Fiancée."

"Yeah. That's what I mean. I seen her. Seen the two of you down by the pier." His eyes filled with pubescent wonder and he shook out his hand like he'd just burned it. "I mean, so she's crazy. Who cares, you know?"

"Okay, Kevin. Make like a gazelle."

"Huh?"

"You can go now."

"Oh, right. Good luck, man."

Unlike all the other times he'd heard that lately, "You'll need it," did not follow. Still it hung in the air, a reasonable inference, as though it had been said.

He sat in his battered Volvo at the mailbox, sorting mail in his lap. The postcard showed a stylized drawing of a coyote sitting by a cactus, howling at the moon. Postmarked Kingman, Arizona.

"Lenny," it said, in writing so familiar it made him ache. "I can't call anymore. It hurts. I couldn't hear you loving me, and I needed it. I kept wanting to ask you to love me louder. I'm losing ground, Lenny, lots of it. I'm real sorry."

He climbed the stairs to his flat, the cold ocean breeze flipping hair into his face. He brushed it back with one hand. Lately he'd been tempted to cut it short again, but it was so thin on top, and he liked to hide in its shagginess. He'd thought of coloring out the gray, too, but he felt sorry for men who couldn't accept these things gracefully. Just loose thoughts, rattlings for a change he was never going to make.

He threw the mail down on the counter next to Cruiser, who fixed him with a steady stare. No messages on the machine, but why should there be? She wasn't going to call anymore. It hurt.

He sat on the couch and tried to make a list of

everything he loved about Kid, so he wouldn't be caught napping next time she asked. Not because he wanted a written list, but because he feared anything unearthed might slip away again.

What presented themselves were not so much reasons as impressions, fluttering by like an unsteady heartbeat, like a baby animal frozen in his well-meaning grasp.

Like the baby goat.

But he didn't understand what the baby goat had to do with love, and it had nothing to do with why he called Kate "Kid," that was just a friendly jab at the difference in their ages.

His paper still said nothing, though the reasons swelled uncomfortably in his belly. He drank two beers, a week's supply under better conditions, and tried to nap.

He drove straight through to Kingman, nine hours, and cruised the main drag for a night spot. He found three. The bartender at the first hadn't seen Kid, but stared at the photo and said he'd like to. When Lenny asked if he was sure, he said he'd definitely remember.

At the second, he learned she was in two nights ago, left with a bodybuilder, then came back late, closed the place down, and left with two college boys. Oh, yeah, and she came in last night and left with an Indian regular.

"Sorry, dude," he said, maybe thinking Lenny had been told something unexpected.

He drank a beer and watched the man's face and

wondered what he must be thinking, maybe that those men had something to do with love, rather than danger, that Kid kissed them, and knew their names, that their brief presence in her life was a replacement for Lenny somehow, a reflection on him. He supposed it might seem that way to someone who didn't know her.

His second beer was delivered by the bouncer, who calmly explained that if she came in again tonight, he wanted no trouble. Lenny calmly assured him there would be none.

Kid did not come in.

He lay on the bed in a Motel Six, fully dressed on top of the covers, and phoned his friend Rodriguez, the math teacher.

"Did I get any mail?"

"Tons. You mean any from her."

"You know what I mean."

"Yeah. A postcard. From Needles."

"Needles? Jesus, she's closer to home than I am. Read it."

"It says, 'Lenny, you probably think I'm running away from you, but I'm just spinning in circles. I want to come home but the circles don't let go. I love you, Lenny. I'm real scared for us both.'"

"That's it?"

"That's it."

"How's the cat?"

"Fine. It just stares at me."

"Hey, Rodriguez? You're my friend, right? Go easy on me in the staff room."

"They're not talking about you."

"Liar."

"They're not. The Home Ec teacher is making it with the Principal. You're old news."

"You're kidding. Do the kids know?"

"The kids know everything. Where do you think *we* heard it? Look, Len. Since I'm your friend and all. . . I just have to ask. Why do you do this? I mean, I've seen her. I know why. But, what I mean is, what are you willing to trade off for all that youth and beauty?"

"This is not about youth and beauty, Rodriguez. God. Do you really think that's what this is about?"

"Enlighten me. What's it about?"

Lenny set the receiver on his chest, stared at the motel ceiling, drew a few purposeful breaths. "If you're my friend, Rodriguez, just check the mail and feed the cat. Okay?"

He found her sister Meg's house right where it was supposed to be, on a numbered street in Albuquerque, New Mexico, looking modest but freshly painted, friendly somehow, very much unlike a Motel Six.

Meg answered the door. He knew her from photos, except in real life she looked more pregnant, about nine months more. A blond boy with big doe eyes clung to her sacky dress.

"Can I help you?"

"I'm Lenny."

"Lenny. Oh. You're Lenny. Pleased to meet you. Is Kate with you? Come in."

She led him through a sea of toys, sat him down on

the couch, offered a beer. His brain said no, he had to get back on the road, but he heard himself accept it because he didn't want to leave this place. It was warm and cluttered and smelled of diapers and living things.

Meg said John would be home in an hour, and would want to meet him, and would he mind sitting tight while she put the kids to bed.

The sliding glass patio door stood open, admitting a breeze that barely felt cool, and he stepped outside and turned his face up to the stars, and closed his eyes. When he opened them the stars were still there, along with everything else.

Meg's voice startled him from behind. "Trouble with Kate?"

"She's gone."

"Oh. I'm sorry, Lenny." He felt her hand touch the back of his hair, and he closed his eyes against a rush of warmth. "Is there still time to get your deposits back?"

"What do you mean?"

"Didn't you book a hall and a band for the wedding?"

"Oh, yeah." And a tux. He'd put a deposit on a tux. "You don't think she'll be back by then."

"I think that's what this is about. Don't you?"

She handed him the beer and the bottle felt cold and wet in his hand. He took a long swallow, and did not turn to face her, just talked to the stars.

"I don't know what this is about. We were okay. She was doing really well."

"Anybody can do well for awhile, Len. Even Kate. You know this has nothing to do with you, right? It's just compulsive. If it was cocaine or something, it might be easier."

"I know. I know that. I came here to ask you a question."

"You want to know what happened to her."

"Yeah."

"She never told you."

"No."

"Then I don't think it's my place to."

"Okay. I understand."

"It happened to me, too, is the thing, and our brother Ricky, but he's dead now."

"But you're okay."

"No. I'll never be okay. After fourteen years of therapy I can honestly say I feel much better. But Kate hasn't even told one person. Like the man she was going to marry."

Was going to marry. He played the words over in his brain a few times, thinking they might sting less with practice.

Then John came home, and they sat in the living room and drank another beer together, and John seemed to like him, so he wanted to stay in this place forever, and talk about how they all loved her, and what could be done.

When the chiming clock announced eleven Meg excused herself, saying she was sleeping for two now, and kissed Lenny on the cheek before leaving, and John made him a bed on the couch.

He lay awake thinking this would be a good time to make that list, because the reasons felt close to the surface and well-ordered, but he woke at first fight, and the list remained empty, and he hadn't even known he'd been asleep.

Meg came out in her housecoat and made him the best cup of coffee he'd had in weeks, and he sat at her kitchen table under the scrutiny of two blond children.

"I hope I'm right," she said, brushing fine hair out of her eyes, "to not tell you about it, because if you knew how bad it was, you'd know what you were up against. And then maybe you'd stop killing yourself and go home."

"Let me get this straight. You think if I really understood how she's been traumatized I'd stand back and let her drown."

"Oh, Lenny," she said, and hugged his head against her shoulder. He closed his eyes to the feeling, and when he opened them he watched one of the children hit the other repeatedly with an oatmeal-coated spoon. "Lenny, I don't want her to go down any more than you do. But she's going. And she's taking you under with her. So I'm thinking you might want to let go."

He finished the last of his coffee in three gulps and pushed away from the table. To stay in this place would be to invite the logic of that statement to settle in.

Meg walked him to the door.

"When I run out of air," he said, "I'll let go."

She gave him a hug, her big belly pushing him away as she held him close. "Do the women of the world a favor, Lenny. Have yourself cloned."

Then, halfway down the walk to his car, he thought he heard her say, "If you survive."

Rodriguez read him another postcard, this one from Gallup. "I'm trying to stay in this one place, The

Elkhorn, but it won't work forever, Lenny, it never does. Maybe if I could see you it would all come back. I want to come home so bad."

He arrived in Gallup at five p.m., and sat in The Elkhorn nursing club sodas, purposely not asking the bartender if he'd seen her, or with whom.

At nine p.m. he was joined by a fortyish woman, reasonably attractive, with dark red hair, who sat down uninvited and announced that he was not the kind of guy she sees at The Elkhorn.

He switched to beers and told her a great deal about Kid, hoping to make it clear that he could not be picked up, but every statement seemed to backfire.

"You wanna dance, honey?"

"No. I don't dance."

"You really love this Kate, huh?"

"Yeah. I really do."

"Why?"

"That's a good question. Nobody ever asked me that before."

He walked to the bar for another beer, detoured to the men's room, but she did not go away. He sat down with her again and told her about the baby goat, just to hear it out loud.

He explained that he'd only been six years old, and the goat only two days, and he was fascinated by it because it was afraid of everything, and he knew he could make it not be afraid of him. So he chased it around and picked it up, and it just froze in his arms, didn't try to struggle, and it thrilled him to feel that little heart drumming against him. He held it and talked to it and petted it, and then set it down. And it ran away again. Like it had never known him.

"I mistook fear for indifference. I couldn't see it as the nature of the beast. I'm older now. Wiser."

"Wise enough to know that freezing in your arms isn't love?"

"I don't want to talk anymore."

"Good. Let's get out of here."

He looked into her eyes and noticed their greenness for the first time, and allowed himself to be struck by the idea that she might hold him if he went home with her. But he might miss Kid. No, it wasn't even ten. He needed to come back later.

They left the Elkhorn together, and wove their way down the dark street, and his brow furrowed wondering what she'd expect from him, and how he would address those expectations.

And then he saw her. He could have passed the alley with his head turned away, but he didn't. He saw her. Pressed against a dark man in a dark leather jacket in a dark alley, her long blond hair pinned up in his hand, their faces close. He froze, and the red-haired woman walked a few steps without him, then stopped and wisely came no closer.

He watched the dark man pull her in for a kiss, and Kid slam him up against the brick building, and slap his face, and he swung on her with a fist but she ducked her head and rammed it into his belly. He expected her to look up and see him watching, breaking the moment, but she did not.

He tried to run to her, but the red-haired woman grabbed a handful of his sleeve. He turned, wrestled with her, argued that the man was hitting Kid, but got only a look of pity in reply.

"They're not fighting now, Hon."

Lenny looked down the alley again. They were not fighting. Their bodies ground together in a slow, heated dance, and he needed to turn his face away. Needed to get back to the car. Thought he needed to throw up, but then he never did.

He sat in his car and stared at the mouth of the alley, which did nothing. He made a fist and slammed it down on the steering wheel, and it hurt much more than he expected.

He rubbed it for a moment, then said, "Ow."

The woman stood on the street outside his car, but he didn't look at her, because her face would say she felt sorry for him. He looked back toward the alley.

What the hell was he doing? He jumped out of the car, powered by something he'd never felt before and did not understand. He turned the corner into the alley with his eyes closed, his only concession to fear, and shouted for her, a bellowing karate yell, a noise that mustered all his energy and sent it blowing out again, that frightened him with its velocity and command.

"Kid!"

A moment of silence, then he opened his eyes. What he saw was worse than anything he could have envisioned on the back of his closed eyelids.

What he saw was an empty alley.

Back home, he faced his deepest fear—that he would not remember what he had done before her, that his life would contain nothing of moment.

But the days were not entirely uneventful. On the second, he discovered he had lost his deposits on the hall, the band and the tux. On the fourth, Cruiser ran off and chose not to return. And on the day they had chosen for the wedding, he received awkward consolation calls from two friends.

On the fourteenth day, he heard a knock that sounded muffled and soft, like a little bird hitting a window. He knew before he opened the door. She didn't come in straight away, just stood on the welcome mat brushing dirty blond hair out of her eyes.

"Did you lose your key?"

"No."

"Are you coming in?"

"Can I take a shower?"

"You live here. Remember?"

He stepped back and watched her walk by, and smelled her walk by. She smelled like tobacco smoke. He didn't dare reach out for her, because she'd gone wild again.

He put the lid down on the toilet seat and sat on it while she showered, focusing all his hope on a milky image through the stall door.

"Cruiser ran away."

"How long's she been gone?"

"Week and a half."

"She'll come back. She always does."

When she turned off the water and stepped out he handed her the biggest, softest towel, and she stood before him naked and dripping and toweled her hair. He noticed that every one of her fingernails had been bitten deeply below the quick, leaving her fingertips wounded.

"Come here," he said, and she did.

He took ointment out of the medicine cabinet, and a box of Band-Aids, and motioned for her to hold out one hand.

"I gotta wear ten Band-Aids?"

"Look, this one's infected." He touched her middle finger and she flinched, but silently. It was blue and swollen in a way that only an abscess under the fingernail could explain. "We'll have to soak this one. . . see if we can draw it out."

"I missed our wedding. Huh, Lenny?"

"Maybe that was a bad idea." He smoothed ointment on the tip of her thumb and peeled a Band-Aid. "Maybe we shouldn't rush things."

She pulled her hand away. "Don't be sure you want me back, Lenny, don't decide yet. I have to tell you some really bad stuff about where I've been."

To his surprise, he realized that he hadn't decided yet. He reached his arms out and she stepped in, still dripping wet, and pressed the side of her face against his chest.

"Start at the beginning."

"When I left?"

"No. The beginning. You were a little girl. And weird, scary stuff kept happening."

"I don't talk about that."

"Then you might need to make a new plan. Because I can't keep doing this."

Several minutes passed in a silence marked only by her grip, which prevented him drawing a full breath. He wanted her to cry, but she didn't.

Then she lifted her head and explained that it was a pretty long, involved story, but he said that was okay. He said he had plenty of time.

DANCING WITH ELINOR

1. MADAM PRESIDENT

The things I like to do are the things I do well. Consequently, I hate to fly.

I was standing at departure gate A23. In front of a TV tuned to CNN. Enjoying watching Elinor. A satellite shot of Elinor swirling over the Atlantic. Headed obliquely for D.C., my destination. She might only be a tropical storm by then. But now she was 111 miles per hour, moving at nearly 15. Now she was 350 miles across, with gale-force winds 200 miles out from her eye. She was one gorgeous motherfucker of a storm. And I was stuck at a connecting airport, outside my real life. And I enjoy that. A lot.

I also liked this girl at my left. We stood nearly shoulder to shoulder. Taking the image in. Together. The way strangers can be together. Only at a time like this, though. After a minute she lifted her cell phone and made her first call. To the person who would meet her. If and when we ever reached our destination. Her significant other.

How did I know that? It wasn't hard. Because she didn't say hello. She didn't say who was calling. She just said, "Hey." Hey, as in, it's me.

Then she said, "This could take a while."

And, "I have no idea. I'm playing leapfrog with a category four hurricane here."

And, "As long as it takes, I guess."

I was immediately reminded of the one about dancing with the eight-hundred-pound gorilla. I wanted to say, "We're not done dancing until Elinor says we are." But I didn't want to frighten her. Don't spook the locals. Though truthfully she might not have fallen into that category.

Despite my thinking of her as a girl, she was probably mid-thirties. And yes, that does depress me. How women that age look like girls to me. But we were not the same animal, she and I. She was close to six feet, with a looseness to her limbs. She was all denim with hair all down her back. Not curly, not straight. Just disorganized. But a disorganized that worked. I hate to admit there is such a thing, but there you are. She was not tight, or neat, or compact. Or in control of everything. So if I'm a woman, she has to be something else. So I called her The Girl.

Just before she hung up the phone, she said, "Susan. Wait. Don't hang up yet."

And she looked over at me. Saw I was listening. Met my eyes with defiance. Dared me to make something of it. Dared me to disapprove. When I just stared back, she took the phone to a more private location.

I pulled out my cell phone. Turned it off. Wanting to be even farther from my real life.

The interesting thing is that I knew she had a problem on the other end of that phone line. But she didn't know. Not yet.

There were other calls over the next seven hours. Though I only heard her side.

What do you mean you haven't told him yet? I'm halfway there for Christ's sake. How can this not be the right time? This is the time we agreed on.

Well, I hope so. Because I'm on my way and all. All my stuff is in storage. Hell of a time to get cold feet, you know? There was a time to consider all this, but it's over.

Yeah, but she's a grown woman.

Yeah, I know you're her mother. But she's not a child. That's what I'm saying. She's a grown woman. She'll deal with it.

Because people deal with things.

Well, I hope so. All my stuff is in storage. I'm halfway there.

Okay. Good.

No. No, Susan. No way. If you can't bring yourself to tell him by then, just don't come. No, that won't work. I'm not going to a hotel. And I'm sure as hell not staying there. This is the deadline we agreed to. What makes you think it's going to get easier later on?

No. I don't. I think it's just a goddamn hurricane. I don't believe in omens anyway.

Don't even use the storm as an excuse. You're not looking at that direct a hit. You're not out boarding up your windows. Don't even try to sell me that.

Well, while the two of you are flood-proofing the basement is a great time to have that talk.

I mean it, Susan. Don't come to the airport if you haven't told him. I'm serious.

Well, I sure hope so.

Then, upon flipping the phone closed, she'd again look defiantly into my eyes. Daring me to disapprove. Why she thought I'd disapprove, I don't know. Force of habit on her part, maybe.

She was squirming on that awful bank of airport seats. Trying to get comfortable. She had those endless legs propped up. But not for long. She took them down. Stretched out her lower back. Took off her denim jacket. Under it she wore only a narrow tank. A heather gray ribbed tank. I ran my eyes over the slimness of her shoulders and upper arms. She must do yoga. Could be she worked out, but that tends to make you tighter. More bound up. This was a long look. Lots of freedom of movement. But strength, too. I'm an admirer of necks, shoulders. Upper arms. Collar bones.

She met my eyes for the hundredth time.

At first she offered up the usual defensiveness. The practiced challenge. Then you could see it dawn on her. Finally. She caught on. And it had been right there all along, too. It was easy. But it took her so long to see what was right in front of her.

I could almost look into her eyes and see the word form in her head.

Oh.

It's like that. Oh.

I could tell she'd been happier the other way. She

was easy with defending. Now she clearly felt uneasy. She chose to handle it by talking.

She said, "My feet are swelling up. And I can't keep them up much longer, because it's killing my back. I'm almost desperate enough to lie down on the floor. But not quite. I mean . . ."

She looked down at the floor.

I couldn't see her feet or her ankles, but I took her word. She wore jeans. Boots. I wore nylons, a skirt. Open shoes. But I also use diuretics when I travel. I know all about bloating. It's one thing to fly when I fly poorly. It's another thing to look puffy doing so.

I continued to consider her upper body.

I could feel her wanting to put the jacket back on. I could feel her pulling away. Much the way she might if I ran a hand along those shoulders. Not just eyes.

I said maybe I could get them to break out some cots. They have them. All airports have them. She said she hadn't known that. "Well, they're not cots in the best sense," I said. "Just slings. But they *are* horizontal."

I went off to pressure some hapless airline employee. I believed I would get cots. But the best I could get was an offer to break them out if we hadn't boarded by 9:00 p.m.

When I got back she'd put her jacket back on.

"It's going to be a while," I said. "You look like you could use a drink."

"I'm fine."

But not really, she wasn't. She had been changing seats. To avoid inane conversations. I could tell. I hate them, too. I could see them eat into her brain. Wear her down.

"I was just thinking. It's quiet in the Admiral's Club lounge." That's what I said.

"You can't get me in there."

"Why can't I?"

"Not for free."

"So?"

I watched her work that over. Maybe I'd go through this whole thing—pay her way in, buy her lunch and drinks—and maybe she'd go sit by herself. No one to say she couldn't.

In my head I silently repeated the word. Quiet. Bait cast into clear water.

"What the hell," she said. "I got time. Huh?"

Yeah. That was probably the key factor. She was willing to sell a piece of her time for thirty-five bucks plus drinks. Probably not because that was so much money for her. Probably because she had so much time.

We sat at a table in the bar area. On soft, padded armchairs. I think she knew I'd buy her a drink and a sandwich. She didn't say so. But I offered. And she hardly seemed surprised.

She ordered a tequila. By now it was late afternoon. But I expect she'd have had one for breakfast if necessary. The look on her face said so. There were no rules at this juncture. No wonder I love this so much.

I thought she might just sit there for hours and not say a word. But it was only minutes. Then she looked at my face before speaking. And looked away again.

"I don't understand why people live in something that's not the truth. Or anything different from how they want to live. I don't get that. Why they don't just say what's true."

I said I'd like to second the motion, but couldn't. I understood.

"Explain it to me then."

But there's a mile gap between what you understand and what you can explain. And I said so.

She nodded. Like she'd anticipated no more satisfaction from the day. Or from me. "I don't know what you're expecting from me."

"Nothing," I said.

"Good. Just so we're clear."

And after that we somehow took everything back off the table. Went back, magically, to the land where nothing had ever been said out loud.

We talked about the storm-chaser sides of ourselves. All we can find to love in a hurricane. Nothing about who we are. She had the walls up on that score.

A lot of the time we didn't talk. She put her feet up, sipped her drink. Closed her eyes.

After all, I had promised her quiet.

Later, I found her in the ladies' room. She stood at the sink, washing her face. Looked at me in the mirror. As though she'd never expected to look up and see anyone else. As if she were adjusted to the intrusion of me now. A necessary evil. She did not look at my eyes, though. Instead, she scanned me up and down. A distant assessment.

I told her we had cots.

"Ah," she said. "Good."

I could tell she was in no mood for camaraderie.

I took the cot right next to hers. Sat on the edge of it. Behind her. They'd set them up in an unused gate. At the far end of the concourse. No real direct light. I felt her gear up to speak. Knew whatever words she mustered would push me back a step.

"You again. Life is full of coincidences."

It was a cut. I should've let it be. Let it alone. But I didn't. I said, "We make judgments. Who we want to be close to."

Then, I kicked myself right away. I stepped too far just as I told myself not to move.

She spoke over her shoulder at me.

"She might still come. You know that, right? She could still be there."

So, that put everything back out on the table. That I'd been listening to all her conversations. And she knew it. That I was treating her like she was up for grabs.

That she wanted me to stop now.

I took a big step back. "Of course. I'm sorry."

I might've just moved away. Permanently. Or I guess I mean somebody else might have. Instead, I admired our ability to communicate. And negotiate. It was worth the price of admission, just to watch us work.

It was after eleven. I lay on one of the cots. Looking at her back. I could hear someone snoring. I could hear her make one more call.

Susan.

We're still hoping sometime tonight.

Well, I can't. I don't dare. Believe me, I'd love nothing better than an airport hotel. But they might board in two hours. Or they might push it back another two.

I know. Me, too. But you still haven't told him, right?

Yeah, well, that's true either way. Somebody'll get hurt either way.

Yeah, I really mean it. Don't come to the airport if you haven't told him.

I'll just go home.

Well I hope so.

Then she clicked off. But I didn't know it for a time. She never said goodbye.

Many minutes went by, maybe an hour. I thought she was asleep. She turned over to face me. But with her eyes closed. She looked too vulnerable. Wrapped in her jacket, tightly, like she was cold. Or just exposed. I sat up and draped my coat over her. Lay back down.

A while later she opened her eyes. Spoke to me in the dim.

I didn't wonder why. And when it showed itself to be something more trusting, I wasn't surprised. Because she was in between. And, unlike me, not enjoying it. She'd packed up her old life. And the new one was disintegrating underneath her feet. So what did she have with her, in this in-between?

Only me.

"Even my blue lines are gone."

My gut held still. Tight. Waiting. Knowing she was telling me something that mattered. I didn't ask what she meant. She would say.

"You know how a sheet of paper always has blue lines. Even if there's nothing written on it. It's like the formatting on a computer disk. But even the blue lines are gone."

I told her I enjoy that, though.

"Not me."

Then they called our flight. Announced we were finally boarding for D.C. I couldn't imagine worse news. People applauded. What the hell were they thinking? What's wrong with people, anyway? The things they find amusing, I'll never understand.

Since it was all over now anyway, I turned on my phone. Just long enough to learn that seven new voicemail messages had accrued. At least five would be Martin.

I turned off the phone again. I would tell him the battery died. Whether he'd believe that or not, I didn't know. Or care.

2. THE GIRL

I made a lot of mistakes that day, but mostly on the inside, where nobody needs to know but me. Like, for example, I let myself believe that when we finally got on that goddamn plane, the nightmare would be over, and I could stop holding my breath. Instead, I got an aisle seat next to one of those idiot men who sits with his legs splayed apart, using up half my leg room. I know, it doesn't sound like much, but try to cross-reference it with the exhaustion and the other obvious emotional pressures. Sometimes you can take it and sometimes you can't. It's a resistance issue.

One of two things happens to you on a day like that. Either you develop a sense of altruistic community, or it makes you combative. I planted my feet, literally. I refused to move my leg, even though he was leaning on it. Two minutes in, my left leg was already trembling, and it was a four-hour-plus flight to D.C. You get the picture. Hopefully you do.

I was thinking what an idiot I was to get on this plane. To fly all the way back east to see what Susan decided. Why didn't I call her one last time, tell her to save me the trouble if I was coming for nothing? But I froze in the desperate thought that a little extra time could make all the difference. And in that pathetic moment of my indecision, they closed the cabin doors.

Then I looked up, and there was that woman, standing over me.

In my head I'd taken to calling her Madam President. Because I'll be damned if I was going to ask her name, and you have to call somebody something. In your head I mean. It was because she looked like a politico. The first time I saw her, I pictured her taking the stage at a Democratic convention, staring down the crowd and telling them she was twice the man her opponents would ever be. Daring them to look her in the eye and say it wasn't so. I pictured her as the first viable woman presidential candidate. I believed she could make me vote for her. I did not believe she would end up borderline stalking me. That didn't go with the image.

"Nobody likes the middle seat," she told the guy with the big wide legs, and he looked at her with aggressiveness, probably wondering why she would torture him by pointing that out. "How about if I trade you?" She handed him the stub of her boarding pass, and he eyed it like a used car he was too smart to be tricked into buying.

"This is in business class," he said.

"Your lucky day."

"Are you nuts?"

No one had yet asked my opinion about any of this.

"I want to sit with my friend," she said.

And Leg Man made himself scarce.

This was a moment of big-time ambivalence for me. On the one hand Madam President was the only familiar thing in my world. I mean, in the bizarro world of this disaster. I mean . . . what do I mean? I mean if it's true that all we have is the here and now, then Madam President was all I had. On the other hand the hypervigilance was making me tired. I wasn't sure that—at a purely emotional level—I had four hours of it left.

At first we didn't talk. She thumbed through the Sky Mall catalog. Ripped out a page or two and stuffed it in her overly expensive looking attaché. Crossed her nyloned legs and let one drift way too close to mine. But she didn't say a word, at first.

We didn't talk until nearly an hour in. By this time the cabin lights had been dimmed to allow people to sleep. The guy on her left was snoring, his face smashed against the window. Just when I thought I could let down and not hear another challenging word from her, she hit me again. I should've seen it coming. An aisle seat in business class doesn't come cheap.

"So, do you think she'll be there?"

I was so surprised by the question that I actually looked her in the eye. "Now how would I know that?"

"You know," she said.

"I don't. Of course I don't know. I don't know what you're talking about. How the hell would I know?"

"In here," she said and almost touched me.

She extended one hand toward my solar plexus, the source of most of my discomfort. But she didn't touch me. Not quite. But I tightened the muscles there, guarded myself against her touch. Reacted to the touch of her energy, which jumped the two-inch gap. She spoke quietly, because just about everyone on that plane was either asleep or trying to sleep.

"In here people know things. Where you stand with everybody. What they mean by what they say to you. And the part of you that says you don't know? That's just your brain overriding what you know. Because you don't trust it. Or because it's not the answer you want."

I took a deep breath and sank into depression. Just like that. Just as fast as I would sink in water if I didn't try to save myself. Only it didn't feel like I was sinking into it, it felt like it was rising up around me. I breathed again, drew it into my mouth and nose, my lungs. I didn't fight it anymore. I felt how hard I'd been clinging to believing I couldn't know yet, not until I got there. How important it was not to know. For a little bit longer. Just to live in Maybe Land for four more hours. It almost felt good to let it go.

"I don't really feel like talking," I said.

I sat breathing in my doom for five or ten minutes. I guess it was that long. Then I made the only outward mistake of the day. Only maybe it wasn't a mistake, I don't know. I want the moment to do over, but maybe not everything you wish you could take back is a mistake.

I was just sitting there, looking down at my own legs. Looking at my left hand, drooped over the end of the armrest. And beyond that was her crossed leg, the inside of her left leg, bare except for her nylons. It was just an inch or two from the outside of my fingers. So I moved my fingers over an inch or two, and I touched her calf. Right almost at the back of her knee. Then down, following the curve of it with the outside of my fingers. I didn't look at her face, not at all. Not once. I just focused on the calf. Like it existed unowned, or at the very least would never rat me out. For those couple of seconds, it was all about that one curve of calf. I think she might've stopped breathing. Then I ran out of reach, and I took my hand away.

I know why I did it, but I don't know if I can explain. I did it to change the way I felt, the same way I might walk by an ashtray and pick up somebody else's cigarette and steal one hit, even though I don't smoke anymore. But right at that moment, you need something to change the way you feel, and you'll take anything.

And it worked, too. It filled me with this nondepressed static electricity. Not a sexual electricity; it was more about fear. It was more about the danger, the audacity, the complete and utter outrageousness of touching a total stranger. It was better than what it replaced.

And then, when I was done, I set it right back down in the ashtray, because it was a cigarette I had never intended to smoke. I just wanted that one spectacularly ill-advised hit.

I sat back and closed my eyes and kept them shut, tightly shut. I refused to look into the eyes associated with that calf. Call it cowardly, call it what you will, but I wasn't going to do it.

After a minute I felt her lean closer, felt her breath close to my ear.

"I'm going to the restroom," she said. And she climbed over my legs, briefly bracing a hand on one as if for balance. As if.

I sat with my eyes squeezed shut, full flight-or-fight raging in my belly, and let the ambiguity of her simple statement terrify me. Did she mean, I'm going to the restroom, and I'll be right back? Or did she mean, That's where I'll be, come meet me there? Could so easily have been either one. I let confusion rattle me for as long as I'm guessing it would take her to walk ten steps toward the rear of the cabin. Then I remembered what she said. About knowing.

I leaned out into the aisle and craned around to look. She was standing at the restroom door with her hand on the latch, and we looked at each other. Except the cabin lights were off, and we were a long way apart by then. She actually stood in a spill of light from the flight attendants' area at the very rear of the plane, but that only lit her from behind and threw her features into shadow. And yet we froze for a time and watched each other. So what were we watching? Silhouettes frozen, I guess. The body language of frozen.

I shook my head.

I thought it might be too subtle a gesture for the subtle lighting, but I was wrong; she got it all right. She dropped her head and opened the door and went inside and that was that.

I sat back again and squeezed my eyes back to shut. She was gone a long time. I thought she might never come back to her seat.

When she did she climbed over my legs, but without touching me. Turned off her overhead reading light.

"I just . . ." I said, but I didn't know the end of the sentence, so I clammed up again. What did I just? I didn't even know. A few seconds later I said, "I guess I just don't get what the point would be. Total stranger, someone you'll never see again." Of course I was whispering.

"I would think it would go without saying. Something outside your real life like that. Something that's just so. . . outside your real life."

I laughed, but it came out as more of a snort. I leaned in close and looked into her face in the dark and realized I wasn't afraid of her anymore. And realized I'd been afraid of her before, all in the same moment. Afraid because she could play that card at any time, but now she had, so she had no power over me. Now I might even get to lead.

"Here's a news flash," I whispered. "This is your real life. That smokescreen you're making sure I never touch, that's the fake. This is the real deal. Right here."

I expected her to counter with something clever, but she never did. That was the last we spoke on the plane.

Amazingly, I slept. But I was startled awake by a bang of something hitting the bottom of the plane. Based solely on feel, a mountain range.

"Jesus, Mary, and Joseph," Madam President said on an outrush of breath. I had a feeling she'd have said something smoother, given more time to prepare.

Then the plane righted itself and bumped a few more times, and I swallowed my stomach back down and adjusted to not being dead, or even dying. I don't understand how turbulence can create that sound and feel. How it can hit the belly of a plane with that force. It's just air. I know it can, but only intellectually. Really, I don't get it.

The pilot came on and apologized for "the wake-up call" and said a few other things, but in a southern accent so thick I only caught every third word. But he said to buckle our seat belts. And that it was rough. Thanks for clearing that up.

We dipped again, suddenly enough that I lost my stomach, like on a roller coaster or a mountain road, and I heard a few people gasp a lungful of breath, and Madam President was one of them. I sat back and rode it out. I have a perverse enjoyment of stuff like that.

I looked left and saw her squeezing the life out of both armrests, and I could tell it was no game for her. That's when it hit me that she's not a good flyer like I am. And I had a strange thought. Maybe she hadn't sat next to me to play games. Maybe her little obsessive pursuit had nothing to do with it. Or not everything to do with it, anyway. Maybe she needed to be with somebody. Maybe, just for that moment, I was all she had.

I checked with my gut, but I never got a clear read on the answer. But I reached over and put my hand on top of hers. At first she just kept her death grip on that armrest. But I edged my fingers under her palm, and in time she turned her hand partway over, opened it up a little bit, and allowed it to be held.

3. MADAM PRESIDENT

Not that I think of myself as the easily affected type. God knows I'm not. But it broke my heart to see her standing in that no-man's-land of airport where people get met. Among the black-suited mercenaries holding up signs. Just standing there, taking in the nothing.

I went to the baggage carousel. Not because I didn't want to help. Because I knew she didn't want me to.

After a while she came over and watched the bags go round and round.

A few minutes of that and I moved closer to where she was standing. Shoulder to shoulder, like at the start. Only this time it was just baggage. Swirling.

Outside, rain splattered off the roof of the covered walkway. Onto travelers running for cabs and town cars. Now would come the messy part. The cleaning up.

"I was hoping she'd be here," I said.

First she didn't answer. I was giving up thinking she would. Then she said, "Thanks." That's all. Thanks.

I asked her where she'd go.

Another short answer. "Home."

I wanted to tell her she wasn't entirely right in what she'd said on the plane. A little bit right, maybe. But not as right as she might think. Tell a lie long enough and you own it. Lie or no lie, it's mine. And that makes it my real life. But she'd throw that back in my face,

I think. Because she's one of those who takes things more head on.

Besides, it was too late. She spotted her bag. It was big. It rolled. She hauled it off the belt. Pulled out the retractable handle. Towed it away from the outside doors. Away from ground transportation. Back to the departing-flight desks.

I watched her to see if she'd look back. She did. I waved, but she didn't even raise her hand to wave back. Just nodded once. That was okay, though. That was akin to just saying "Hey" when you call someone on the phone.

I think I liked that even better.

KID TREES

A few weeks before Zach showed up I stole a pocket knife from one of Mom's revolving-door visitors. He accused me of it but I denied it, planned to go to my grave denying it, and she backed me up. And that was it, he was gone. So long, Charlie.

No great loss.

I took it up in my tree and carved a smooth spot for my cheek. I had a branch that I lay on like a momma lion. Okay, a girl lion. I saw one in a film at school, lying on a big limb, straddling it, all four legs hanging down. I could do that. Except momma lion had a tail that twitched, while the rest of her looked plenty relaxed. If I'd had a tail, I think it would have hung down like the rest of me. I wasn't feeling twitchy that summer.

With my cheek on that cool stretch of bare wood I could monitor the house without feeling as though I was any part of it. Either nobody caught on to where I was, or more likely, they didn't care to look. I mean, the less commotion in that house, the better.

The day before Zach turned up Mom set the couch on fire with a cigarette. I think she might have had too much to drink. She didn't drink all the time, but boy, when she did, she did.

So I was lying awake that night, which was not so very unusual in itself, and I smelled the smoke, and when I got out to the living room, the very first little flame shot up. I ran some water in a pot and threw it on the fire. It splashed all over her face, and she came around, and boy was she pissed.

So I said, "Hey, what was I supposed to do? You set the goddamned couch on fire!"

She slapped me. Normally she used all kinds of cuss words, and she didn't care if I did, too, but I had to leave God out of it.

She looked kind of pathetic, lying there all wet with that damp cigarette butt in her hand.

She had a perm that summer, and she seemed to think it looked great, but it always ended up flat in some strange ways where she'd been lying on it. She had gained a lot of weight and she was wearing one of those lime green polyester things that made her look like a pale avocado.

I think she must have caught that in my eyes, because she snapped at me and told me to go back to bed, but I went out to my tree. After awhile I fell asleep up there. When I woke up, I decided it was a good spot to spend the summer.

I had some compadres that summer, to hang out in the trees with me, or at least I thought I did. Richie, and Snake, whose real name was Morris.

Richie was a year younger and Snake was one older than me.

We'd carve guns out of dry wood and play bandit games in the little aisles between the neighbors' garages. They were just worthless bits of yard that nobody used, but it sure pissed people off to see kids in there.

The girls in the neighborhood were pretty rough on me. Called me Tarzan girl and said I was uncivilized. But, you know, consider the source.

Still, I took off when I saw them coming.

When we got bored of everything else we built a tree house up there. In my spot. Just the three of us. When Zach showed up he wanted to help, first thing. He almost climbed up in the tree with us, because he said we didn't look like we were doing so good. We weren't. But under no circumstances were grownups allowed in that tree. Kids only.

Zach sat on the back stoop and popped a couple of beers and stared up at us. He looked skinny and strange to me, like somebody I'd never met before, even though he'd been hanging around for a few days. Still, they didn't last long, so there's no need to get attached, it's like naming a cat you don't get to keep.

It was just a little platform when we were done, and pretty rickety at that.

It rocked when you walked over to the right-hand side. It had an egg-shaped hole in the middle that Snake cut with his father's keyhole saw, and stairs made of two-by-fours nailed to the trunk like ladder steps, so you could stick your head right up through the hole as you climbed.

I called down to Zach that any grownup who stuck his head up through that hole might get whacked, and I held up the left-over two-by-four to drive home the point.

He just laughed and gave a little salute.

Then Mom came out and told Richie and Snake to get lost, and told me to get in the house, pronto, and I got slapped for talking to her boyfriend like that.

"Boyfriend," I said. "Ha. Is that what we call them now."

I could see by her face that I'd gone way too far.

She came charging like something out of a nature film on Wild Kingdom.

I thought I was dead. Before she got to me, Zach grabbed her around the waist and told me to go to my room while she cooled out.

She broke his grasp and stomped out of the house, and I knew she'd be back in about three hours with an armful of bags of new clothes, which meant the lights and the water were as good as gone for a month.

I looked at Zach and he looked at me. I figured this was the part where I was supposed to say, Oh thank you, oh aren't you cool, which pissed me off.

I said, "This is all your fault. Everything was fine before you got here."

It wasn't, of course, but maybe he'd be stupid enough to believe it. God knows all the others were.

Zach took me for a ride on the back of his motorcycle so I wouldn't hate him. See how these things pay off?

He had on a black leather jacket, and that was cool, but it was the only thing about him that was, the way I had it pegged.

Well, okay, his boots were cool. I wanted ones just like them, but I knew Mom would have a fit, because she thought I didn't dress enough like a girl. I mean, who would want to?

Anyway, I wouldn't hold on to Zach, because that's too creepy, it's not like I was his girlfriend or anything. I held that little strap that goes across the seat, but there was nothing behind me to lean on, and when he put on the gas I felt like I was going to blow right off the back.

And boy, could he put on the gas. Once I got a peek at the speedometer and we were doing eighty-five. Just at that moment I think I might have understood what Mom saw in Zach.

What Zach saw in Mom, now that's another story altogether.

He took me out the old reservoir road, and the leaves on the pavement did this little woosh thing as we came by, kind of turned a spiral and ran away.

When we came around the curves the bike leaned over until I thought our knees would scrape the pavement. At first I was afraid to lean with him, because I thought the bike would dump right over, but it didn't, and I started to get into it.

Scary but cool.

I got to watch black and white cows hanging out in front yards, and barns that looked like a good wind would take them down. Old combines and tractors rusting just where they had broken, and avocado trees, and persimmon trees.

Mind you, I'd seen all this before, but these things don't really come through the car windows. They suffer in the translation.

And the fence posts seemed to rush by like they were under their own steam, and I decided, without being able to put it into words, that life is about perspective. Like a farmer standing in a field and a kid racing down the road on a Kawasaki, arguing about whether the fence posts are rushing by or standing still. Each thinking the other is crazy or blind or both, neither willing to give up until the other sees the light.

I was only twelve at the time, I wouldn't have put it in quite those words, but I felt it and it stuck.

We got off by the reservoir, which was good, because my butt hurt. I wouldn't have said so.

By that time I was thinking this Zach was a pretty cool guy but then he took off his helmet and it was back to geek city.

What do you expect of a guy who just got out of the Army?

He had hair a quarter of an inch long, with little ridges where the helmet had squashed it down, and his face was sort of shiny. If he hadn't been six foot four he wouldn't have looked much older than me.

Actually, I think he was only about ten years older than me, which made him the same age as Kiki.

We had three kids in my family. Kiki, who was

twenty-two that summer, and whose real name was Loretta, me, and Todd, who was almost two. Mom used to say, yeah, well, once every ten years whether I need one or not. Everybody thought that was funny.

Except me.

Zach lit a cigarette.

I said, "Hey, don't I get one?"

Then we had the usual go-round, wasn't I too young, wouldn't my momma mind, and I went around with him, but I knew he'd give me one, because he wanted me to like him.

As it turned out, he even lit it for me. I took a couple of puffs, and inhaled the first one to impress him. I knew better than to do that all the way down.

First thing he asked me is why I was such a tomboy. Why did I always wear those baggy black sweatshirts and those jeans all ripped out in the knee?

I shrugged and started skimming some stones on the reservoir. I was wishing he would get to the speech. He got to it soon enough.

"I know it's a little hard for you to accept me," he said, "me being so much younger than your mom and all."

I shrugged and skipped another stone.

She'd done worse, I was thinking. I was dizzy from the cigarette but it wouldn't do to let on.

"I know you don't like me."

I shrugged and let fire another stone. Good one. Five skips and then that nice little plunk.

"I love your mother very much," he said.

I took a drag on the cigarette and looked him dead on. I didn't doubt him for a minute.

"She won't let you."

It was something Kiki had said. I hadn't asked what it meant, because it sort of explained itself. But I couldn't have explained it.

I told him Mom doesn't want a man to be happy with, she wants to have one disaster after another. It's a distraction. Kind of like a bill consolidation loan, where you combine all your debts and make one monthly payment, only this was problem consolidation.

I'd heard that from Kiki, too.

He screwed up his face and said it didn't sound like something for a twelve-year-old to say, and maybe somebody was putting ideas in my head, and maybe that somebody was dead wrong.

I said, "I'm older than I look."

He laughed the way grownups do when they say they're laughing with you. Only I'm never laughing.

"You know what it reminds me of," he said, "when I see you up in that tree?"

I shrugged and braced for the worst.

"It reminds me of a story I wrote in high school. Haven't thought about it for years, but I think about it all the time lately. It was about these hordes of little kids who just sort of. . . packed up and split. The girls launched out to sea on boats, and the boys climbed up in trees. The Coast Guard went out looking for the girls but they were gone. And the fire department put ladders up into the trees but they were empty."

I dropped my cigarette and completely forgot to look cool. "Gone? Like, for good?" It seemed almost too good to be true, even in somebody's imagination.

"Yup. Forever. The teacher didn't like it, though."

"Figures."

"She said she didn't understand it. Where did I think these thousands of kids had gone? I said, 'Well, some place that's really a whole different world. They just went somewhere different.' You know what she said?"

I shook my head in a kind of stunned stupidity.

"'What's wrong with this world?'"

"But she was kidding, though. Right?"

"Don't know. To this very day I haven't figured that out."

"She must have been kidding."

"She only gave me a C+."

I shrugged and skipped another stone, the spell broken.

"Grownups," I said.

"Yeah. Grownups."

I held on to Zach on the way home.

After that I decided that the tree house needed to be more livable, more long-term.

So I got Richie to take a chair up there, which wasn't easy, and we hung blankets to make it like a tent. For more privacy, you know?

But that turned out to be too much of a good thing, because Snake, who was thirteen, started getting big ideas. Said he and I could be doing it, we were old enough.

I said I'd heard all about that and nobody was old enough as far as I was concerned.

Even if I'd wanted to do it, I don't think Snake would have been the guy. I was looking for somebody a little more like Zach. Snake looked too much like a bulldog. He had this flattop that he thought was cool, and he was kind of chunky.

As he squatted in the tree house ragging on me this little beam of light came through a hole in the blanket, right over his head, and made him look like he was wearing a halo, which just didn't fit.

Then he started making fun of the fact that Mom and Zach were doing it.

I said, well, I wasn't really so sure. I was, of course, I mean, it was pretty obvious, but I just didn't feel like going on about it.

Then Richie, the little squirt, the one who couldn't even keep his own nose clean, he said, "Your mom does it with everybody."

So I decked him.

I just spun around and slammed him one, only not quite the way I like to remember. I like to think it was a nice roundhouse punch, but really I'd never thrown a punch in my life. I just gave him a shot to the nose with my elbow. It wasn't pretty, but it worked.

He stumbled backwards with blood squirting out of his nose, hit one of the hanging blankets and took it down with him. All the way down he was swinging his arms like he could get his balance, like there was still time not to fall.

I remember the sound when he landed.

He never ratted on me, but word got around with the kids in the neighborhood that his broken nose and his broken arm were both my handiwork, and from then on I was poison and nobody would hang out with me, not even the guys.

If I'd had it to do over, I'd have done it just like that again. Maybe thrown a cleaner punch. Some things are worth their price.

After things started getting bad with Mom and Zach, and the fights were mostly an every night thing, I spent about six days up in the tree, alone, pretending I might wake up in a whole different place.

All the time I knew it was stupid, and that I was too old for that crap, but something about it being Zach's idea made it seem a tiny bit less than impossible.

The night he left I woke up when his motorcycle kicked over. I climbed down fast, but he was out the driveway and headed down the street.

I ran after him for almost two blocks, yelling his name as loud as I could, even though I knew he couldn't hear me.

My throat hurt, and my lungs were ready to burst, and besides, the neighbors were turning on their porch lights and coming out to see. So I just waved my arms in case he looked in his rear-view mirror, but I should have known he had no cause to look back.

I kept thinking if I could just get on the back of that bike I could disappear with him. Then he turned a corner and he was gone.

I asked my mom where he went, and where I could write to him, but she said she didn't know and she didn't care. That's when I knew I was stuck.

After that I didn't come down much, until the night I did.

Mom got drunk and had the T.V. up real loud, so I never came in the house, I just slept up in my tree.

And I guess I must have rolled over to the right-hand side, because I heard this crack, and I was flying through the air, still too much asleep to get the message.

Landed real hard on my left side, broke my collarbone and my leg, I found out later, and my only thought at the time was that I was owning what I did to Richie.

Payback's a bitch. Grounded for the rest of the summer.

I don't mean grounded like my mom said I had to stay home. I mean grounded, as in on the ground. No more getting up above it all. And the day after the cast came off I had to go back to school.

That was almost two years ago now, that Zach left. I've gotten a lot more realistic about everything. Like for example there's no magic to this disappearing stuff.

Snake is my boyfriend now, and he'll be sixteen in eleven months, and between the two of us we've got three hundred sixty dollars saved up toward a car.

Problem is I sort of like him and sort of don't, but Kiki and I talk about this a lot, and she says that's nothing new or special. She says we'll get off on our own and somewhere down the road I'll dump him, and that's no big deal either, because guys are only using us anyway, that's just the way it is.

Once I saw Zach at the Woolworth's downtown, but he didn't see me. He was with a lady about my mom's age, and I didn't try to say hi, because I thought it might embarrass him.

He wasn't as good looking as I remembered anyway.

That was just kid stuff.

I'm not a kid anymore.

THE LAST LOUNGER MAN

Shirley breaks the surface of consciousness the way a sledgehammer might break through wet tar. Nothing neat or sudden about it. One cheek is pressed against cold, pebbly concrete, and as she lifts her head she touches painful indentations on her face.

No memory, but that will likely prove a blessing.

To call it waking would be far too euphemistic, and Shirley dislikes euphemism, feeling duty-bound to strict reality, as though she owes it a debt for ignoring its existence in the past.

The man smiles at her, and extends a bottle in her direction. "Morning, Shirl. Little hair of the dog?"

She accepts the offering. A long slug of brandy finds a hollow place in her gut that, so far, can only tremble. It's a ghost of mornings past, waking up with a painful storm in her head and a man who seems to know her. Welcome back.

He sits in the alley beside her, still shaded from the early sun, in dirty jeans and a red flannel shirt, a bandana tied around his head. A cross between a homeless man and a pirate. His back is pressed against the brick of the tavern. He seems at home, undisturbed to inhabit this place.

He looked more respectable last night. But that's a memory. No need to encourage those.

She sits up, gingerly, and presses her back against the cold brick, almost shoulder to shoulder with him. It's a trust thing; he is a drinking buddy, whether that will prove beneficial or not, regardless of how that friendship grew.

Some things drop into your life fully formed. Live with it. A lesson she learned from her AA sponsor, whom she wishes not to think about just now.

She reaches for the bottle. "How do you suppose I got here?"

"Depends on what you mean by here, Shirl. Santa Barbara? This particular alley? This philosophical place in your life?"

Another slug of brandy burns its way down, to find and repair the damage it previously created.

"All of the above."

Before he can answer, she hears it. The metallic sound of its wheels against the tracks. The whistle. It causes her to crumble along preset lines, like a hammer blow to glass that has already sustained cracks and fissures, and held together only by luck and lack of disturbance.

He's talking, but it sounds distant.

"It definitely had some thing to do with a train. You said you had to get off a train because you couldn't go by somebody's house. Some guy. Eric, I think. Something about being in his house watching the train, not the other way around. I didn't quite get that part."

"No," Shirley says. "Me either."

Then she politely excuses herself to be sick in private.

She brings the man back to her hotel, by cab, not for any immoral or even humanitarian purposes, but because she drank all his brandy. She owes him.

It's not quite eight a.m. as they hit the hotel bar for bourbon and waters. The bartender is not the same one who asked Shirley to leave last night, to her relief.

The man raises his glass in a toast, but never says what they might be toasting.

She downs her drink and orders another.

It has nothing to do with feeling good, which she no longer expects. She has dropped below a centerline, where good cannot be reached, not by any imaginable stretch. The trick is to reach for stable and holding, and, having found it, to try not to let it go.

He looks around as though surveying Heaven or Eden. "Pretty classy, Shirl."

"The Miramar?"

"Well. I guess it's all relative. You don't remember my name, do you?"

"I was never good at names."

"Jim."

"Of course."

She sees the bartender watching from the corner of his eye. She hopes he's mostly watching Jim, the dark, muscular miniature of a man who might almost be called a bum, though certainly an imaginative version.

Then again, she might not look or smell much better

herself.

She finds excuses to leave.

They stroll out across the tracks to the boardwalk, and sit on plastic lounge chairs still wet with morning fog. Shirley closes her eyes to wait for it. She won't watch, only listen.

"I can't figure out if you love trains or hate them," Jim says when the whistle sounds in the distance.

"No. Me either."

"I like them myself. Haven't ridden one for years. But they look good going by. Something classy about a train."

"They look better from the outside."

The whistle sounds again, just behind them, a long series of warnings, and Shirley squeezes her eyes shut and tells herself to hold on. The way she might talk to a child.

Don't cry, Shirley. Hold on.

Then the sound fades, like everything else.

She does not wake up, rather regains consciousness. The outward surroundings seem an improvement, but, she reminds herself, that is only outward.

Jim sits in a chair by the window, legs crossed, looking out over the pool, his beard gone, his hair clean. He wears only a towel wrapped around his waist.

She measures and judges the clean-shaven face, dark and friendly, creased with use. The bandana has been used to hide male pattern baldness. Like that matters. If anything, it's nice to hang around with someone her own age.

He looks back and sees she is awake.

"Don't get the wrong idea, Shirl. I'm not planning to overstay my welcome. Dry clothes, I'm gone."

"Why don't you call room service, Jimbo. Get some food up here. Couple of shrimp cocktails, maybe. Steaks to follow."

He smiles as he waits on the line. "My ex-wife used to call me Jimbo."

"Don't get us confused."

"If I did I wouldn't be here."

"You probably didn't deserve her."

She hears the remark hit the carpet, clumsily. A bowling ball of a thing to say. Where on earth did it come from and how did it slip past the guards?

"True enough, Shirl. Yeah. Room service? Two steaks and two shrimp cocktails. And maybe even a bottle of champagne." He catches her eye and she nods. "Okay, well, in half an hour then."

He hangs up the phone.

"Twelve noon it starts."

She wants to apologize but it's gone, floated by in peace, and she hates to dredge it up again.

She digs in her purse, finds her wallet. Flips through credit cards. Chooses the Visa, because it's less than five hundred dollars short of maxed. Holds it out to him.

"What's that for?"

"Clothes." Every seemingly generous move on her part a clumsy apology, usually for a less identifiable transgression. "We have to get you looking like you belong here."

"Why, are we here for awhile?"

"'Til the plastic runs out."

"Gee, thanks, Shirl."

"It's like Confederate dollars. Only as good as the institution behind it."

"You must have been pretty good to get all that credit."

"Emphasis on the past tense."

"I didn't mean it like that, Shirl."

"True enough, though."

After lunch she naps, and Jim comes back in a gray Italian suit, with a gold stud in his left ear. He brings flowers. He has decided they should go dancing.

Jim dips her often as they dance, to the delight of the crowd that has circled the floor. Shirley knows they have drunk just enough to carry a crowd, to symbolize release, and that they will drink more, and their approval rating will be lost. She enjoys it while she can.

"So what was wrong with Eric?" he whispers in her ear.

"Nothing was wrong with him."

Her body has lost the looseness that works, that collects envy. The dance has become stiff.

"So why'd you throw him over?"

She pushes away from him and finds her way back to their table, where champagne waits patiently on ice. The crowd finds other things to do.

In a moment he sits down beside her. "Sorry, Shirl."

"He was a lot younger than me."

"So? I'm younger than you, but we can still cut a rug."

"The hell you are. How old are you?"

"Forty."

"Forty?" In her own voice she hears rudeness, a claim by tone that he looks much older.

"It's like a car, Shirl. I'm not old in years, just mileage. How old are you?"

"None of your damn business," she says, and breaks for the door, wobbly but determined.

Another younger man. Damn it. It's a curse, it knows where you are, it finds you.

By the time she flags down a cab, Jim is at her elbow, looking dashing, like a leading man from a romantic fifties movie. "Let's not spoil a good thing, Shirl."

She likes the feeling of his arm around her waist, and he climbs into the cab after her, and she lets him. After all, it's a party. Streetlights flash across his face as they ride, and she smiles at him, and hopes he can't see, because the smile feels hopeful and shy and other things she doesn't want it to be.

She asks the driver to stop at a liquor store, where she buys two more bottles of champagne. Jim says she's his kind of woman, which she knew. After all these years, she knows whose kind of woman she is.

Back at the hotel they drag lounge chairs down onto the sand, and Jim pops the cork on one of the bottles, and it flies into the surf.

"To an endless party."

He takes a drink and passes the bottle to her.

"Not endless. Just 'til the plastic runs out."

"And then?"

"Then I sober up and go home."

"Sober? What's that?"

It seems like a serious question to her, demanding a serious answer, though she knows he would disagree.

She digs in her purse until she finds her keys, throws them in his lap, and he singles out the medallion, just as she meant him to, holds it up in the moonlight, and whistles softly.

"Twelve years, Shirl. Damn. Ending when?"

"A couple hours before we met."

"I had one of these once."

"You had a twelve year medallion?"

"No, just a medallion. One year. And some chips for thirty days. About six of them, I think."

"So, how'd you get so far from the program?"

"I'm no farther from it than you are, Shirl. We are both royally drunk."

She says nothing for a time, just stares at the moon, pleased with the accomplishment of keeping it in focus.

Then he says, "How do you know you've got another sober in you?"

"I did it once, I can do it again."

"Ah, but the first one's free, Shirl. You know that."

In the confusing hour after this unpleasant discussion, Shirley remembers falling off her lounge into wet sand. She remembers Jim lying close to her, though not how he got there, and kissing him for a long time, and wondering in a disconnected way why things didn't go further, and if they ever would.

Then it is light, and the tide is in, cold and salty all around them, and all the clothes they wore the night before they still wear, and a handful of hotel employees watch them from the boardwalk, but it doesn't seem like her most important concern.

"What do you mean you can't authorize it. I know my own credit limit."

She is at the hotel desk, attempting to prepay a second week. "Sorry, ma'am," the clerk says, though she hardly looks it. "That card's been reported stolen."

"That's ridiculous. It's a mistake. Look."

She shows the woman her driver's license, so she can see that the name and the face match, and are clearly hers.

She fishes out another card, and it also comes up stolen.

She can feel Jim fidgeting behind her.

When the last card has been tried, she walks away from the desk with him, thinking he looks less like a romantic lead and more like a man she met in an alley or a bar.

"I should have called my daughter. She's a worrier. And her husband's an attorney. I guess this wouldn't have happened if I'd let her know where I was. She must be frantic."

"Time to sober up and go home then."

She doesn't like his voice. Suddenly they have near nothing, but he has this one thing to hold on to: the knowledge that she has made a difficult promise, and made it sound easy, and now the time has arrived.

She returns to a semblance of life, her back pressed against the familiar brick of the tavern, the air cold and wet with morning fog. Jim has covered her with the rumpled gray jacket of his new suit. His eyes look sad, in a way she never imagined they would.

"I dreamed you offered me a little hair of the dog."

"Would if I could, Shirl."

"How did you stay drunk before I came along?"

"Oh, I had ways. A little panhandling sometimes. Or I'd hang out near a liquor store and offer to buy for the underaged. For a bottle. If they were stupid I'd go out the back door with both. If they were smart they'd be waiting back there."

Shirley pulls her knees up to her chest and hides her face between them. She feels overpowered by the need to get out of this foggy glare, shower, and down two bourbon and waters. That a shower is beyond her means seems impossible to grasp.

"Jim, I can't live like this."

"Then I guess you'll be sobering up and going home."

After a difficult pause, Shirley digs through her purse for loose change.

"Don't suppose you can get much for two-ninety."

"You suppose wrong, Shirl. The world is full of cheap wine."

"Should I be waiting by the back door?"

She expects him to look cut, but he doesn't bother.

"Nah. You're my buddy, Shirl. I wouldn't run out

on you."

While he's gone she decides she isn't really homeless. She owns her very own house, in San Luis Obispo, the trick is to get to it.

I'll call my daughter, she thinks, but she's given the last of her change to Jim, who arrives back with a bottle of wine, which they split, and is gone too soon, and doesn't feel like enough.

Sometime near sunset, Shirley opens her eyes to see a familiar figure standing over her.

"Mom. My God."

"Valerie. How did you find me?"

"Your credit card trail was pretty clear. God. Mom, we've been sick with worry."

"Well, as you can see," she says, sweeping her arms wide to indicate her surroundings, "there was nothing to worry about."

Valerie does not look amused, and when politely introduced to Jim she neither says, nor looks as if, she is happy to meet him.

Shirley sits up, confused by her surroundings, then remembers she's in a motel room with Valerie in Carpinteria, where she's been for almost three days, drying out. Preparing for home.

Valerie says, "I called Eric. He wanted to come down, but—"

"Oh, God, no, Valerie. Please."

"He's been worried sick about you, Mom. We all

have."

Shirley wants to run her hands through her mangled hair, but it seems pathetic to even evidence concern for her looks, so far beyond immediate repair.

"He wants to know why you left him like that." Another silence that Shirley refuses to fill. "We're trying to understand, Mom. Really we are."

"But you don't understand."

"Not completely."

"No," Shirley says. "Me either."

Valerie's car idles smoothly at her back as Shirley carries the grocery bag into the alley. She's sure Jim has moved on, that she won't find him, and can't decide which she hopes will be true.

He's just as she left him, except in his old jeans and flannel shirt, and bandana around his head. His eyes come up, startled, like a deer at a watering hole, but soften quickly.

"Shirl. You look positively respectable."

She sinks into a sitting position beside him. "Where's your new suit?"

"Right here," he says, holding up a bottle of good bourbon.

She shies away from the fumes of his breath, not in revulsion, but fear of temptation. He isn't too drunk to notice.

"Well, if I had someone to come pick me up and take care of me while I dried out, maybe I could look respectable, too."

"I'm glad to hear you say that. Let's go."

He seems to dissolve into himself. "Go where, Shirl?"

"Home."

"Where's home?"

"San Luis Obispo. What's the difference? This isn't it."

"I can't, Shirl."

"You had a year medallion once."

"No, I made that up. I had the thirty day one, though."

Shirley stands, leaving the bag on the concrete. She reaches a hand down to him but he only studies his shoes.

"Your ride's leaving, buddy."

"Shit, Shirl, if I could do that would I be doing this?"

"I brought you some food. I'll just leave it right here."

"You know I'll trade it."

"Guess there's not much I can do about that."

"Guess not."

"I put my address in the bag. Don't trade that away."

"No. I won't."

He braves a glance at her, but briefly.

"So long, Jimbo."

"So long, Shirl."

She walks far enough to hear the steady, comforting hum of Valerie's waiting car, without once looking back.

"Hey, Shirley. Don't leave a light on for me."

She say she won't but it's a lie; she will. For awhile. Not forever.

REQUIEM FOR A FLAMER

I got a roommate. Dave. Most of us don't have roommates. Most don't want them, I guess. Most have some family they brought here with them, but me and Dave, we're waiting for word on all the family we ever had.

Dave lost a wife and two daughters. They already identified his wife and his older girl. He's just waiting on that other daughter. Every time the hotel desk phones up to our room, I get scared they found his little girl. Then he'll go back to Denver to make his arrangements.

Arrangements. That's a funny way to put it, I think. I wouldn't usually talk about it that way. But you pick up those words here. They teach you to talk like that. Me, I'm not a real eloquent guy. Not really smart or anything. But you pick it up, start thinking it's a normal way to say a thing.

The other thing that seems weird—when the phone rings, how come I don't get scared they found Marlene? Maybe I am, but I don't know it. Most of what I feel right now I don't feel. The only thing I know for a fact is I'm scared Dave'll go home.

Marlene was my fiancée. She is the only one I lost. Then again, she's the only one I ever had. I never even had a lot in the way of friends, until now.

I have two really big problems right now, other than the obvious. Dave going home is one of them, and the other is so bad I can't even say it. I can't always put words to things like some people. But I'm scared Dave'll be gone soon, so I decide to tell him now, while I still can. Dave might know what to do.

I'm awful glad the airline paired me up with Dave. I think most people don't want a roommate during this because they don't want strangers to see them cry. But Dave is not a stranger now. We are like Army buddies. We been through a war together. We are in the trenches, me and Dave, right now.

Besides, we don't really cry. Dave hyperventilates. I mostly stare off into space.

He just sits there on the edge of his bed and listens. I need him to believe me, because maybe if he thinks I'm gay he won't want to room with me. That would be worse than if he went home.

"I always liked women, Dave. Ever since I can remember. And just because I tell you what I'm about to tell you doesn't mean I made any exceptions for anybody. You just have to understand how it was with me and Marlene."

Nobody understands that. I never gave anybody a chance to try.

Dave's a young guy but his hairline is receding.

And his face is old. All of our faces are old. Maybe we'll start life over again, and get young, like we were before this happened.

Or maybe not.

He knows this is important, what I'm trying to say.

"Just because Marlene wasn't born a woman doesn't mean she wasn't a woman. I wish you could've known her, Dave. She was a lady. Too good a lady for a guy like me, I'll tell you. Every guy I ever knew thought I was the luckiest sonofabitch on the planet. And, you know what, Dave? They were right. Guys used to turn and whistle at her on the street, and I knew they were thinking, how's this guy get so lucky? Woman like that."

After I say all that I start to hyperventilate. Which is funny, because I never did before, not in my whole life. I guess I picked that up from Dave.

He comes over to my bed and sits with me and gives me his brown paper bag to breathe into. That means a lot to me, that he'd let me touch his bag, not like he's thinking I probably got AIDS or something. He has brown eyes that look really sad. Since I met him, his eyes always look lost. Losing his wife and two daughters makes Dave lost, but my story makes him sad.

"Don't take this the wrong way," he says while I'm breathing into his bag. "It doesn't matter to me. But just so we know what to do. Did Marlene already have. . .you know. . ."

"She was gonna have the surgery, in a year or two. I'm not a rich guy, though. We were saving up."

"I just asked because I was wondering about the

Coroner's Office."

"Yeah, I'm wondering about that too, Dave. I thought maybe you'd know what to do. I don't want Marlene being a laughingstock. I don't care what they say about me. But Marlene was a classy lady. I don't want anybody saying stuff, you know, calling her names. Like when I was in high school they would've called Marlene a flamer. I don't want to hear bad names, nothing said against her, you know?"

My voice starts to break up and Dave puts the paper bag up to my mouth.

"Breathe, Jerry, breathe into the bag."

"It's gonna get around, because they're not gonna know if they got the right body. There'll be questions. I thought you might know what to do, Dave."

"Breathe into the bag, Jerry," he says, and this time I do.

"I think you need to talk to the Coroner right now. Before any questions can be asked. Before they find her."

I drop the bag on the floor, and Dave picks it up and holds it in his lap like it's some fine china or something.

"I don't know if I could do that, Dave. I never told anybody. Not one single soul. You're the first one ever. But, the Coroner, I don't even know him, Dave. Not like I know you."

"You want me to go down there with you, Jer?"

"You'd do that for me?"

"Sure I would. Something to do. That would be good."

I know what he means about that. There's nothing to do here. Everything you ever used to do, you forget how. It's like your life just stops. Or you stop, and your life keeps going. Like when you step out of a car while it's moving. First thing you do is fall down. Takes a while to get clear on what just happened to you. But, like I said before, I'm not a real eloquent guy. I'm probably not explaining it right at all.

The Coroner is a very busy man.

They actually tell us that. Like we're not two of the people in the world who know it best. The man they send out to say this garbage is not even the Coroner's assistant. He's what they call a spokesperson. Somebody from the County who talks to the families, and the press, and tells them the Coroner is doing the best he can. The guy is really tiny. Maybe five foot four if he's lucky. I feel like I could pick him up and break him like a stick, but I am not a violent guy, really. It's just the stress that makes me think like that.

The whole thing makes me remember that scene in The Wizard of Oz, where they get to the castle but the little guy says they can't see the Wizard, no way, no how. Nobody gets in to see the Wizard. I know that probably sounds really strange, that I should think about that now. But my brain's been doing this a lot lately, going back to things from the past, from when I was little. I feel little these days.

Dave saves the day. He tells the spokesperson that I have information about the body of Marlene Ashbury that will save the Coroner time. That seems to be the password here, and Dave is smart enough to know it. The Wizard wants to hear that the witch sent you. The

Coroner wants to hear you can save him some time.

My hands are shaking. When was the last time I ate something? I ask Dave, but he doesn't remember either. I'm starting to feel funny, like I might pass out. So I sit down, but that doesn't help. If there was a window in this office I'd open it. There isn't, though.

The Coroner himself comes in. He shakes our hands. I wonder whether he wears plastic gloves touching the bodies. He's part Chinese, I think, and very businesslike.

I give Dave a look that says, I don't think I can talk to this guy, Dave.

Dave puts his hand on my shoulder. Boy, am I glad he did that. Thank you, thank you, thank you, Dave, for not being scared to touch me.

I open my mouth but I'm surer than ever now that I'm going to pass out.

The Coroner wants me to start talking. He is a very busy man.

Dave gets things started.

"My friend has some important information, but it's a difficult thing for him to talk about. I promise we're not here to waste your time. If you could be patient with him for a minute, so he can get his thoughts together."

As soon as Dave says that, I realize he's exactly right. My thoughts are all apart, scattered around all over the place. "My fiancée. . .wasn't exactly. . ." My voice doesn't sound right. It doesn't sound like mine. "Well, I mean she wasn't. . .really. . .well, no, she was.

Really. But I mean, she wasn't born. . .yeah. That's it. She wasn't born. . ."

"Wasn't born what, Mr. Hill?"

"Female."

"I see."

"She was on hormones. So, her, you know, upper body was female. And she had hips. So, like, in some ways you'll look at the body and go, okay, right, twenty-four year old female. But not all the way, you know?"

The Coroner doesn't seem too upset.

"So, what you're saying, Mr. Hill, is that in identifying the body of Marlene Ashbury I will encounter a combination of male and female physical characteristics."

See, now *he* is an eloquent guy.

"Basically, yes."

"That *is* significant information, then. You were right to come in."

"Just one more thing, Sir." I say it fast because he is half out of his chair. "I was hoping this didn't have to get all over the place. I mean, you know how much press there is around the crash, and I'd hate to read about Marlene on the cover of some sleaze rag in the supermarket, you know."

He looks at me funny. "My job is to identify the bodies, Mr. Hill, not to sell information about them."

"I know that, Sir. Really. I never doubted you. I just figure, you got an office full of people. Assistants and stuff."

Now his eyes look sad, like Dave's did. Not as much, though. "My staff understands that the casualties of this disaster are to be handled with dignity." Then, just when he's at the door, he says, "When your fiancée's remains are brought in, I'll remind them. If that would make you feel better."

"It would, Sir," I say. "It really would. Thank you."

After he leaves I tell Dave that was the hardest thing I ever had to do in my whole life. Dave says I did fine.

He asks me if I want to get drunk tonight and I say hell yeah.

Now we're back in our room at the hotel. I'm on my bed and Dave's on his. It's funny how much this place feels like home. Compared to where we just were.

Dave's got the bottle. Some kind of brandy that tastes like fruit. He leans over to pour me some more and almost falls off his bed. So we laugh. Which is, like, strange. Laughing. We forgot what it even sounds like.

"You wanta know something weird?" I say.

Dave says, "Okay. Tell me something weird."

"The part of Marlene that was, you know, like, not what a woman would have? I never even saw it."

Dave doesn't say anything for a minute. "Were you waiting till you got married?"

"Oh, no. Hell, no. We had a sex life all right. Great one. I'll tell you, Dave, I never had it so good. Marlene always wore this really cute little underwear. You know, stockings and garter belts, really sexy things, and panties that were, like, split in the back." The room gets real quiet for a long time and I think, oh shit, why did I say all that? "I'm sorry, Dave. I bet that was more than you wanted to know."

"So she was really feminine."

"You can't imagine. The other women I knew, they were truck drivers compared to her. It was like making love with one of those models from the Victoria's Secret catalogue. She was, like, the perfect woman. Well, that sounds funny, huh? She was perfect except for that one little thing. Pretty big little thing. But she was something. I'll never find anybody like that again, Dave. That's for damn sure."

"Mind if I ask you a question?"

"Shoot, Dave."

"Did you know, when you met her?"

"No. You wouldn't know. You'd never know to meet her."

But Dave knows that already, because I showed him pictures. And he showed me pictures of his wife and his two pretty girls. Lots of times. I saw so many pictures of his wife and his little girls, it's like I lost them myself. I wonder if Dave feels that way about Marlene. I hope so.

"No, we dated for awhile. And I fell head over heels in love with her. Everybody said she'd dump me, 'cause she was way too good for me. But she fell in love with me back. After she told me. She fell in love with me because I was the only guy in her life who didn't know right off the bat and didn't leave after she told him. How about that? We found something worth loving about me. I'm not a smart guy, and I'm not real good looking, but I had that one thing I could give her that nobody else would. That means something, right?"

Dave is nodding and crying. I thought he never

cried. I guess we all will, by and by.

"Yeah, that means a lot, Jer."

"Still, though. I wish sometimes I had a wife and a couple of daughters. That'd be a nice way to go, Dave. I think I would've liked to have just a regular family like that."

Dave nods a minute longer. I think he's really in the cups now.

"I wouldn't've minded making love to a Victoria's Secret model, though. That's not a bad way to go, either."

"We had some good times," I say. "I can't lie about that."

In the morning there's another press conference. Dave and me, we're kind of hung over, but we decide to go.

It's boring. It's nothing we didn't know.

All the newspapers and all the TV stations are here, and they have to start from the beginning, telling about how the lake bed is soft and mushy and ate up most of the wreckage. Like there's some fool somewhere who's been in a coma or something and hasn't heard already.

I keep looking to see where the cameras are. I don't want to get my face on TV. I'm afraid somebody will put a caption under me. Man who lost his fiancée. Something like that. And then when I get home my mother'll call, to find out how I could be getting married and she didn't know.

I lean over and ask Dave if I can see that picture of his family again. He takes it out of his inside jacket pocket. This one he carries with him, but he brought lots. We all did. We all brought albums full of pictures, and we tried to give them to the airline, or the Coroner. And they had to explain that what a person looked like doesn't help now. It's hard to say a thing like that in a nice way, but they worked it out. They know just the right things to say about all the worst ways to die.

In this picture his wife is standing up, smiling. She's pretty, like somebody I'd like. She has blonde hair, and she's thin. She has her hands on the shoulders of the older girl, who's ten. Then the older girl has her hands on the shoulders of the little one, who's only four. They look like a happy, pretty totem pole. The little one has fine blonde hair, and it looks soft. Too bad I'll never get to find out. She's the one they haven't found.

I wonder if she's down in that lake bottom with Marlene, or if they're somewhere else together, and if that helps them at all, that they're together. It helps me.

I start to cry, and Dave puts a hand on my shoulder. It makes me feel like part of his family. That's how they did things in his family. They put their hands on each other's shoulders.

A family would've been nice. Except that's a lot to lose.

Dave and I are getting drunk again. Second night in a row. Nothing ever happens here. Nothing moves. Sometimes I keep looking at my watch, wondering why it doesn't go as fast as it used to. Sometimes Dave starts breathing into the bag and I wonder what he was just thinking about, but I don't ask.

I'm starting to understand how people have drinking problems when they never did before. You always hear people say things like that. "I never used to drink until after the incident." I see now how that can happen. I think after awhile I'll stop, because I never liked the feeling. It makes me so sick. But I can see how somebody could forget to stop. It would be easy.

I wish my brain wouldn't jump around so much. I should just be thinking about Marlene. Instead I think about Dave's wife, Diane. Maybe I can get Dave to give me a picture of his family to take home. Home. That sounds weird. I haven't really thought about home. It's like I'm used to the hotel now. I don't think much about the future.

Dave starts talking. It makes me jump.

"You know, a lot of guys would have beat her up when they found out. If she hadn't had you, some guy might have beaten her to death. That happens."

I know that happens because it happened to Marlene twice. Just not to death. I even helped chip in for some of her plastic surgery. I think it's kind of funny that while I was thinking about Dave's family, he was thinking about Marlene. Kind of funny but nice.

"Well, Dave," I say. "I guess that's the easy way out."

"What do you mean, Jer?"

We are both drunk. It's such a relief.

"Well, if you beat her to death, then you never have to see her again, and then you never have to find out that all those feelings don't go away. Any jerk can use his fists, but it takes a real man to face a thing like that."

Dave nods a lot, for a long time. "Absolutely," he says. "You are the real article, Jer. No doubt about it."

Six o'clock in the morning we wake up to the phone. I'm real sick and I hope Dave'll get it. After awhile he does. I sit up. My guts feel all cold.

Dave says, "Speaking."

And I think, good. It's for him.

And then I remember that's the thing I didn't want.

"Okay, thank you," he says. "I'll be right down."

He hangs up the phone and we're both just sitting there on the edges of our beds in our underwear. Dave rubs his eyes. He looks lost again.

"They found Lissa, huh."

"Yeah," he says. "Yeah, they did."

"Good," I say. "That's good. You all get to go home."

After he leaves I lie back down like I'll go to sleep. But I don't. I keep thinking I'll never see Dave again, but then I remember all his stuff is here. He'll have to come back and get it. And then I'll never see him again.

He's gone all day. I never get out of bed. I never change out of my underwear.

When he comes back he brings me another bottle of brandy. I still don't get up.

"Don't forget you want to stop drinking after awhile, though," he

says.

"No, I won't forget, Dave."

He starts throwing his stuff in his suitcases. He has no idea how to pack. Maybe his wife always did it for him. Or maybe he just forgot how. You forget the simplest things. It's strange.

"I'll call you every day."

But he won't. He'll get back to his own life, just like they say you're supposed to.

"You know, Dave, they're saying now that some of the bodies might never turn up."

"Yeah, I heard that."

"I'm glad they found Lissa."

"Yeah. I hope they find Marlene. They will. Sooner or later I bet they will."

"I wonder how long before I'm supposed to give up and go home."

He doesn't answer. I know he feels bad leaving me here.

"I hear they're gonna have a service on the lakeshore after a while. For the ones that don't turn up. It'll be on TV."

"Well, that'll be some kind of closure," he says. That's another word they taught us. Closure.

He comes over near the bed and puts his hand out to me. I shake his hand and we just hold on for a minute. Like a cross between a manly handshake and two guys holding hands. But it's okay, we're family.

Then he lugs his suitcases out the door. I hear the elevator button go bing. I remember I forgot to ask for a picture of his family, but probably he'll send me one. If he doesn't forget.

I lie in bed and think about the time my old dog had to get put to sleep. I stood in the vet office the whole time, stroking his ears. I watched him go. I thought I'd be upset but I wasn't. He just snored, and then he didn't anymore. I thought, that was so much easier than I figured. Then the vet assistant took him away and I just fell apart. Just fucking fell apart.

When I got the call about Marlene, it seemed like something that probably wasn't true. I kept waiting for her to show up and tell me she couldn't get a cab and missed her flight. I felt like I'd been shot up with Novocain all over. Now it's wearing off and Dave is gone.

Six days go by and I don't get out of bed. I just keep ordering room service. I hope the airline is paying for all this, but they haven't really made us clear on that.

Dave called once, two days ago. It was the day of the funeral. They had one big service for his whole family. I wish I could picture that but I don't know who all Dave knows. He was blubbering and I couldn't understand what he said and after a while I let him go.

Dave gave me this brandy, so I don't want it to be gone. That's one good way not to have a drinking problem. I have about two fingers of it left. I'm drinking as slow as I can.

The lakeshore memorial is this morning. I've been thinking I'm not going to go. But now I'm thinking that I have to get up some time anyway.

I take that shower I've been needing. I look in the mirror. I put on a pretty good beard in six days. A good start on one. I had a beard once. Maybe I'll have one again. That saves me shaving, which sounds like a lot of trouble. But I shave my neck and put on a suit and a tie.

The hotel is using their shuttle vans to take families to the lakeshore. I get in with a couple of other families. They all have flowers. Big wreaths and fancy arrangements. I never thought about flowers. I've been in bed.

There's a little girl sitting across from me, and she has blonde hair. I keep looking at her. I want to tell her how nice it is that she's alive. But I need to stop looking at her, so her family won't think I'm some kind of pervert or something. So I look out the window.

I walk around getting sand in my shoes. The press is here, and everybody brought flowers but me.

The little blonde girl wades out into the lake almost to her waist and throws her bouquet into the water. It doesn't go far. It may lap up on the shore again tonight but I guess it's the thought that counts.

There's this kind of big mushy feeling here, like we all have something in common. But it's not true, really. Not for me. What I lost is not the same as what they lost. I wouldn't even tell these people what I lost. They wouldn't get it at all.

I walk out to the highway so I can hitchhike back to the hotel. They will never find Marlene's body, and that's good. I think she would have wanted it that way. That lake bottom took her secret and swallowed it up so nobody has to know. Nobody can call her names the way it turned out.

I stand with my thumb out and after a while a white car makes a U-turn and stops to pick me up. The driver leans over to open the door and it's Dave in a rental car.

He says, "Jerry, what are you doing? You're going the wrong way."

"I didn't know anybody there," I say.

"Get in."

He's got a big wreath of flowers on the back seat. The banner says, "Marlene Ashbury, She was a real lady."

"That's right," I say. "She sure was," and he smiles.

Now I feel bad, because I didn't get my butt out of bed and fly to Denver for his service. Why didn't I do that? I don't remember. I guess I was waiting for news I didn't know would never come.

We sit in his rental car, and watch the people milling around by the lake. More people taking pictures of the bereaved than there are bereaved.

"You didn't have to come back," I say. But I'm glad he did.

"I wanted to come back."

"I missed your service, though."

"This is different," he says. "This is really hard."

The Channel Three News takes some film of Dave and me, wading out into the lake to our thighs, ruining our good suit pants to set that wreath on the water, which is really cold.

I think that's good, that they got that moment on tape. Maybe a week ago I wouldn't have thought so, but a lot has changed in one week. I just think it's something that people ought to see.

We stand there on the shore and watch it, and it doesn't come back in. It gets smaller, real slow, like watching the time move these days. I think it's going out like it's supposed to. We'll know in a while.

I got a brother who lives all the way up in Montana, but he is still my brother.

Me and Dave, we have our arms around each other's shoulders because that's the way we do things in this family.

THE WORRY STONE

The first time I saw Vida I was still enmeshed in that no-man's-land, that numb, foggy shock that follows one around in the wake of a traumatic event. It's a blessing. It really is. You wake in the morning with no orientation. No memory of what was lost. Then it comes back on you like a sleeper wave. All you have to do is get up and wash your face. Then you call a friend and say you got up and washed your face, and your friend says, "Fabulous, Richard. You will survive." No mention is made of the finer details: the day's work, the unbalanced checkbook, the stacks of bills and messages. No one would dare suggest what they later will tirelessly insist: that life goes on from here. For the moment, simply putting one foot in front of the other is a source of pride. It's a blessing. It is. I wouldn't mind having it back.

For a full six days, I didn't drive the forty miles to see Vida in the hospital. First I had to have that small oil leak fixed, and it took the mechanic a few days to fit me in. That one detail I was not about to numb away for later. If some innocent soul were to skid off the road in a fine, early rain—the mist of water sitting on a wash of filmy crankcase oil, unable to soak into the pavement, just pooling there where the rubber meets the road—it was important that none of the oil be mine. That this new disaster not be any of my doing. I was allowed this strange obsession, too. It was part of the no-man's-land. It was my right.

When I arrived at the hospital, her mother was nowhere to be found. I even asked at the nurse's station on Vida's floor, but as far as they knew, she had gone home for a nap. So I was able to let myself in to the girl's room alone, without introduction, which I then realized was preferable. No one watching my face, able to observe that I'd come with an agenda, some indistinct expectation for gain.

I expected her to be asleep, but she sat half-propped up, her dark eyes wide open and staring at me. There was some startling element in them, something wild and intense. I'd expected, I guess, to see her groggy and half-conscious. Just a handful of days after such traumatic surgery—wasn't she on some kind of heavy painkiller? If so, what must her eyes look like normally?

I couldn't imagine she was nineteen, though I knew from her mother's letter that she was. She seemed high-school age, underweight and frail—perhaps borderline anorexic—with dirty blonde hair, which might actually have been dirty, or maybe that was just the look of it. Not really fair to judge a person's appearance as they lie in a hospital bed, but try to stop yourself. She had dark circles under her eyes, a body strangely slack and at rest. Only her eyes seemed fully alive. Only her right thumb was in motion, rubbing an obsessive, repetitive pattern over a small oval object. Above the neckline of her hospital gown I could see the top of the scar: angry, obvious, and raised. It caught and tingled in my stomach and made me feel squeamish, as though I should sit down.

"You're the guy," she said, "huh?"

I didn't bother to ask how she knew. I figured I must be wearing it on my face, entering her room with an expression that only one person in her world could possibly use.

"Yes," I said, and I moved closer and sat down in a hard plastic chair.

I remember a vague sense of disappointment. I'm not sure what I thought I might see, but I didn't see it. Just a stranger, a girl I'd never met before.

She turned her head to follow me with the stare. Her assessment made me uncomfortable, a role reversal I hadn't meant to allow. "Do you believe in love at first sight?"

Without hesitation I said, "No."

"No? No? Nobody ever says no. Nobody is ever cynical enough to say no." Her thumb continued to move in an almost circular pattern over what I had decided must be a worry stone.

"Well, I stand by my answer," I said. "But it's not cynicism. Just the opposite. I have too much respect for love to believe that. I don't even believe in the concept of falling in love—the falling part, I mean. We should all be so lucky that love is something you just fall into. Like, 'A funny thing happened to me today. I was walking down the street and I tripped and fell into some love.' You don't fall down to love; you climb up to it. There's hard work involved. That's why I believe you can't love someone you don't know. Loving someone *is* knowing them."

Then I stopped myself, breathed. Felt half-dizzy, as though I weren't in the room at all, which I'd been feeling a lot those past few days. And I realized I'd said a great deal more than necessary.

"Then I need to know you," she said.

The door to her room swung open, and a woman came in. I knew it was Abigail, Vida's mother. I could tell. I'd known it would be. I jumped to my feet, defensive somehow, as though I'd done something wrong. Her head tilted, questioningly, hoping I would identify myself without forcing her to be so rude as to ask.

"Richard Bailey," I said.

Her face softened, and she threw herself across the room and threw her arms around me. I stood awkwardly, not quite embracing her in return.

In time, I managed to put one hand on her back, a sort of brotherly pat, and she turned me loose. I realized I'd forgotten to breathe.

She was small and short, and had to crane her neck back to look up into my face. Her eyes held too much, and too much of it was for me. I didn't want all that so I looked away.

"You got my letter," she said.

"Yes. Thank you for that."

"I meant what I said, Mr. Bailey, I want you to know that. We are so, so sorry for your loss. We wouldn't want you to think that because we gained from it, we're not just as full of empathy for you."

"I don't," I said. I could feel myself needing to get away. Needing to go back into my shut-down mode. Needing to be home, with the covers over me, and no one watching. I felt unable to carry the moment. I had run out of gas. "I wouldn't think that. As close as you came to losing a loved one, you probably understand better than anybody."

I edged for the door.

"You're not leaving?" she said.

"I have to. I'll be back. I'll come back when I'm . . . I just have to get some fresh air," I said. "Or something."

At the door I looked back at Vida, and of course she was still staring at me. Her eyes were still the only part of her fully alive, her thumb still the only moveable piece.

I'm extremely lactose intolerant. My wife wasn't. So we always kept both kinds of milk in the house. Only, that night we were out of my kind. It's silly when you think about it because I'm a grown man. I'm forty-two years old. I'm not ten. Why do I need to drink milk with my dinner? It's just one of those habit things. All I had to say was, "Never mind. I'll drink water." I've said that about three hundred times since. I wake up in the night saying it. After I wake up, I'm pretty sure I've been saying it in my dream. I could have just had water.

Why didn't I go out and get the milk myself? It was me who wanted it. I'd brought some work home. I was sitting in the living room, working on my laptop, and Lorrie just took it upon herself to slip out and get milk. I didn't know it had rained; it wasn't even enough rain to hear on the roof. I guess it just sprinkled for a few minutes. First rain in a long time. There's some physics thing to that. Later, after it's rained hard for ten or fifteen minutes, the oil washes off the road. But at first—no, how could that be? You can't just hose oil off the driveway. I've tried. But it's something about the first minutes of that first rain. The water sits on top of the oil. Or something. I had it explained once. But I haven't asked since, because I couldn't bear to hear it again.

Don't you think it's strange how we're all driving all over everywhere, dropping little bits of ourselves all along the road? Oil, transmission fluid, antifreeze. Old tire rubber. Leaving trails of discarded us wherever we go.

Well, OK, I guess you'll say our cars are not us. But I'm not so sure. It's like what they say about dogs: they grow to resemble their owners after a while. Only I think—about dogs and cars, both—it's more that we've created them in our image.

Why am I talking so much? I never used to be a man who did that.

Vida's stare greeted me just as expected. I found myself wondering why I'd come back. I found myself wondering what her stare did while I was elsewhere. It was all part of that disconnectedness, that sense that only I existed in the world because everything else felt like a dream.

"My mom wasn't kidding in her letter," she said. "It

really was a matter of about twenty-four hours. I was going to die that soon. You really get a chance to look death right in the face. You know?"

"Is that what the worry stone is about?"

She held it up under the lamp. "Come here," she said. "I want to show you this." I moved closer, not sure what I was trying to see. "See how it's smoother right there?" She indicated the spot with her thumb. Then she held the stone by the edges. I looked closely, but I wasn't sure if I could see anything or not. "I actually did that with my thumb," she said. "Wore away stone."

I touched her thumb. I wanted to feel it, to see if she had a callous. To see what had worn away more of what. Who was really winning. The sudden touch electrified us. Or, actually, maybe it only electrified me. How would I know about her? She did have a heavy callous on that thumb, the kind guitar players have on the tips of their fingers.

"It's like water," she said. I had no idea what was like water. Certainly nothing I could see. "You wouldn't think water could wear away stone. But it does. It just takes its time. I want to see if I can wear a little groove right into the center of this rock. It may take awhile. But I've got time. Now I do."

"I should go," I said.

"Thanks for the heart," she said. It was a surprisingly simple statement in the midst of all that life and death and indebtedness.

"You're welcome."

I drove the forty miles home and stayed in bed for two days.

Do I believe that the heart is really the seat of human emotion? I'm not sure if I do. I'm not sure it was something I'd ever thought about before.

I'd watched a program once, years ago. A handful of people with transplanted organs. They seemed to feel some connection with their donors, the people they carried a small part of inside. A trace memory here, a favorite food there. It crossed my mind that possibly, just possibly, Vida might actually love me. But did I want her to?

I wasn't sure if I did.

Vida called me once from the hospital. It was late, nearly one a.m.

"Did I wake you?" she said.

"What's on your mind, Vida?"

"I was just thinking about that expression 'Where the rubber meets the road.' I think it used to be from a tire commercial. But I had this boyfriend once who used to use it like. . .you know. . . like an expression. He would say, 'Yeah, that's where the rubber meets the road.' He meant, like, the bottom line—what's really at the heart of the matter, you know? And that's another expression I've been thinking about. 'The heart of the matter.' They're both ways of talking about what's really important. I just thought that rubber one was interesting, because of the way the thing with your wife happened."

There was a long silence on the line.

"Well, it certainly is the bottom line at my house," I said.

"Will you come visit me again?"

"Yes. But right now I'm going back to sleep."

"Promise you'll come?"

"Yes."

It was a promise I did not keep. Unless you count—no. You wouldn't count that. The night I drove by the hospital and parked in the parking lot and looked up at a bank of windows, any number of which could have been hers. I was in the act of conscious breathing. Reminding myself of each breath, and longing for the days when I'd breathed quite well, without a thought. There was a small figure framed in one window. Patient, visitor. I wasn't close enough to see. It could even have been Vida; I can't swear it wasn't. But the odds were against that. I don't guess that counts as a visit.

I also saw her one day on campus, a week or two after her release, walking with two friends. I told myself I'd only come to make sure she wasn't smoking. I'd lain awake all night wondering. What if she was a smoker? How dare she be? I didn't give her Lorrie's heart to abuse. How could she have so little respect? So I just went by to indulge that potential outrage, I suppose. What better did I have to do? I hadn't quite made it back to work, though my answering machine was littered with messages from coworkers and superiors suggesting it might be that time after all. Instead, I went to the college. Truthfully, it was more than one day.

I don't think she smokes. I don't think she saw me.

I don't suppose those count as visits.

Vida showed up at my house without notice. It was about six weeks later. I hadn't expected to ever see her again. And I was OK with that. So far as I could tell.

She stood in my doorway in a shabby, oversized trench coat, her feet bare, her bright-red toenail polish half chipped away, the worry stone in her right hand, her thumb working it smooth.

"How did you get here?" I asked. "Does your mother know you're here?"

"I'm almost twenty years old. You act like I'm a child. Can't I even come in?"

I stepped back away from the door. She cut a straight path to the opposite wall, where the pictures of Lorrie loomed like a shrine. I think I'd been adding nearly one a day, but sadly, I was running out of new additions.

"Wow," she said, "that's weird. She doesn't look at all like I expected. I thought I knew just what she would look like—that she'd look familiar, not like a stranger, you know?"

I wanted to say, Now you know how I felt when I first saw you. I didn't.

She went on. "'Lorrie,' huh? My mom told me her name was Lorrie. That's an OK name. I hate my name. It's weird."

"You know what 'Vida' means, don't you?"

"Of course I do," she said.

"Then I would think you'd like it."

"Know why she gave me that name? 'Cause I tried

to die the first night I was born. From all my heart stuff. She was trying to make sure I never pulled anything like that again."

Transplant statistics rattled around in my brain. How many patients, by ratio, would still be alive in five years. How many in ten. Quite possibly I was remembering the numbers all wrong. But the message in my brain felt clear.

Vida turned off the light. I thought maybe she just didn't want to see the pictures of my late stranger-wife anymore. The only light left in the room came from the lamp in the corner—more of a glow than a light.

Vida let her coat drop to the floor. She was naked underneath. I wasn't entirely surprised. Part of me was. The part of me that was surprised seemed to be under scrutiny by the part of me that wasn't. She looked painfully thin. Her breasts were small and hard, like unripe fruit. So different from Lorrie, whose breasts had been full and soft, a little drooped, like overripe fruit, sweeter and more promising. After that comparative observation, all I could see was the scar.

I walked to where she was standing, picked up the coat, handed it back.

"I'm not going home," she said.

"Put on your coat."

She did, and then locked herself in my bathroom for the better part of two hours.

When she ventured out again, I was sitting under the glow of the corner lamp, reading a World War II novel. She stood over me, all full to exploding with her own deficiencies, whatever they may have been.

With a flip of my head, I indicated the couch, where I'd laid out a pair of Lorrie's old pajamas.

She took off her coat and threw it on the back of the couch. In my peripheral vision, I could see her look back to catch if I was watching.

I didn't watch.

She put Lorrie's pajamas on and tucked herself in under the blanket I'd left on the couch.

By this time, it was close to midnight.

"Why are you being so cold to me?" she asked.

I put my book down, took off my glasses. Pressed my eyes shut and squeezed the bridge of my nose, the way I always do when I'm trying too hard at thinking. It's as if I'm trying to focus all my confusion in the bridge of my nose, but I don't know why.

"I can't afford to lose anything else right now. Can you understand that?"

"No," she said.

And I found myself thinking, No? No? Nobody ever says no.

"I set myself up for loss all the time," she said. "Over and over."

"Well. Women have a higher pain threshold. About nine times higher, I think. It's for the purpose of childbirth, but I suppose it comes in handy for all kinds of things. I just lost my wife, Vida. Just a couple of months ago. Can't you cut me any slack for that at all?"

"What if I waited?"

"It takes years to get over a thing like that."

"What if I waited years? What if a couple years

down the road, I was still right here, waiting? A couple years is a long time." She held up her right hand, stone and all, her thumb still smoothing. "Maybe I could even wear down you. You think I don't see the way you've been watching me?"

"I was just checking up on the heart," I said. "Making sure you weren't smoking, or eating burgers and fries every day."

"You're a lousy liar."

"Well," I said, "I guess I haven't had enough practice."

About an hour later, I knew she was asleep because her thumb stopped moving and the stone slid from her hand.

I stole over to the couch and sat on the edge without disturbing her. I pulled her blanket down a little. Then I placed my ear lightly against Lorrie's old flannel pajamas and listened. I closed my eyes, to block out everything that wasn't right. All that remained was the feel of the flannel on my face and the sound of the heart beating against my ear. But it still wasn't quite the same. Many a night I'd set my head down on Lorrie's chest. I knew how it was supposed to sound. Slow and confident and healthy. This beat was quicker, as if unsure of itself. As if needing to remind me that even the most minute details had undergone change.

After a few minutes, I felt around for the worry stone. I found it half-fallen behind the couch cushions. I placed it in the pocket of Lorrie's pajama top.

I wondered: if I had taken Vida up on her offer and

made love to her, would she have taken a few minutes off from her battle against rock? Or would she have held and worried that stone the entire time?

I rose and called Abigail, and asked her to please come collect Vida and take her away.

We stood over her, watching her sleep. We still had only the glow of the corner lamp, but I didn't want to turn on a light for fear of waking Vida. Whatever she was about to say as her mother led her away, I wasn't anxious to hear it.

"Who belongs to the pajamas?" Abigail asked.

"She can just keep them," I said.

A strained minute, then Abigail said, "Where are her clothes?"

"I'm not sure that's a story you'd enjoy hearing."

Abigail wandered over to the Lorrie wall, and stood with her back to me.

"I guess she thinks she loves me," I told Abigail's back. "Maybe it's not so strange. When you consider all the circumstances."

"Don't take this the wrong way, Mr. Bailey. Not to diminish you one bit as a man, or a human being. But my daughter has a lot of emotional problems. Always has. She thinks she loves a lot of men. Every couple of months she meets a man and decides it's love at first sight."

I felt a pang of loss when she said that. Just what I swore I could not afford. But it moved through me and I was left standing, so I suppose I could have been wrong. I realized with no small surprise that I'd believed, for just a moment, that Vida had seen something special in me, loved me the way Lorrie had, through Lorrie's eyes or with her exact same heart. Maybe I'd thought Vida would still be there years from now, waiting for me to come around. So there was the loss, and I felt it. That's when I knew I'd moved beyond the numbing shock.

"Usually the man is twenty or thirty years older," Abigail said. I wondered if she'd said other things in between, and maybe I'd missed them. "Maybe if she had a father, but I don't know. I'm not a psychiatrist. I just know it's like she has some big empty hole inside. She's always grabbing on to something or someone to try to fill it up. Most men are all too happy to take advantage."

She kept staring at the photos of Lorrie all through this speech. I couldn't tell if she was talking without thinking, or looking without seeing, or both.

"I guess I'm not most men," I said.

She turned halfway back to me. Smiled a little. "Then I owe you two debts of gratitude."

"Just take her home and I'm willing to call it even."

"Can you carry her to the car? She only weighs a little over a hundred."

"She won't wake up?"

Abigail laughed. "Nothing wakes Vida. She's just like a child that way. You can carry her snoring over your shoulder like a six-year-old. One part of childhood she never outgrew."

One of many, I wanted to say. But it seemed cruel. Also unnecessary.

I placed one arm behind her shoulder blades, one

behind her knees. She wasn't heavy. She didn't wake up. Abigail threw the coat over her like a blanket.

On the way from my front door to the car, I heard a small tap, something hitting the driveway.

"Get that," I said to Abigail, knowing it was the stone. It seemed a shame to let all that hard work go to waste, to spoil Vida's chance to triumph over solid rock.

I stood in the street and watched them drive away, feeling something pull out of me. It was as if something was being pulled from the center of my gut, following them away down the street. The way someone can take up a loose thread of your sweater and pull, and theoretically you could be left with no sweater. Whether it was Lorrie's heart I felt leaving or the girl wrapped around it, I can't say, but I don't suppose it mattered because I could no longer separate the two.

I figured in the morning I could call a friend and say, I washed my face just now, and last night I let myself feel. My friend would say, Marvelous, Richard. You will survive. Oh, and by the way, Richard: life goes on from here.

I only heard from Vida once after that. On Valentine's Day, she sent me a card she'd made herself. On the front, with colored magic markers, she'd drawn a heart. A real one. Not a valentine heart, but a startlingly realistic organ with blue veins and arteries branching off in opposite directions. Inside it read:

Richard, I guess you were right. It's not such an easy thing after all. More work and less magic. Maybe it's not a neat shape like the ones on playing cards. Maybe if you give somebody your heart, it's this big, gnarly muscle of a thing that's not always so pretty to look at. You know?

I could hardly argue with that.

I saw Abigail once, at a department store downtown. It was only about two years later, but even so, when I asked how Vida was, I braced myself, half-prepared for the worst.

Abigail sighed and said Vida was all right, which I took to mean that her body was fine. She said Vida was living somewhere in Arizona with a guy who was in his fifties, but she didn't expect it to last because these things never did. Not with Vida.

I remember my reaction. I remember thinking: if he breaks her heart, I'll kill him. And I meant it quite literally. Not if he slaps her face or pulls her hair. That didn't incite bloodlust in me. Only if he breaks her heart. So I guess I fell into the trap, like everyone. Confusing a human heart with a valentine heart. Thinking of an organ as the seat of all human emotion. But I guess I was making progress, just being able to think of it as Vida's heart.

Next thing you know, I'll believe the soft, outer skin of a human being can wear away stone.

THE MAN WHO FOUND YOU IN THE WOODS

October 1, 1954

Nathan McCann stood in the cool autumn dark, a moment before sunrise, his shotgun angled up across his shoulder; he insisted that his retriever, Sadie, obey him. He called her name again, cross with her for forcing him to break the morning stillness, the very reason he had come. In the seven years he'd owned the dog, she had never before refused to come when he called.

Remembering this, he shone his big lantern flashlight on her. In the brief instant before she squinted her eyes and turned her face from the light, he saw something, some look that would do for an explanation. She had been able to say something to him. She was not defying his judgment, but asking him to consider, for a moment, her own. You must come, she said. You must.

For the first time in the seven years he'd owned her, Nathan obeyed his dog. He came when she called him.

She stood under a tree, digging. Not digging in that frantic way dogs do, both front feet flying in rhythm, but gently pushing leaves aside with her muzzle, and occasionally with one front paw. He couldn't see around her, so he pulled her off by the collar.

"OK, girl. I'm here now; let me see what you've got."

He shone the light on the mound of fallen leaves. Jutting out from the pile was an unfathomably small—yet unmistakably human—foot.

"Dear God," Nathan said, and set the flashlight down. He scooped underneath the lump with both gloved hands at once, lifted the child up to him, blew leaves off its face. It was wrapped in a sweater—a regular adult-sized sweater—and wore a multicolored knit cap. It could not have been more than a day or two old. He would know more if he could hold the flashlight and the child at the same time. He pulled

off one glove with his teeth and touched the skin of its face. It felt cool against the backs of his fingers.

"What kind of person would do such a thing?" he said quietly.

He looked up to the sky as if God were immediately available to address that question. The sky had gone light now, but just a trace. Dawn had not crested the hill but lay beyond the horizon somewhere, waiting.

He set the child gently on the bed of leaves and looked more closely with the flashlight. The child moved its lips and jaw sluggishly, a dry-mouthed gesture, as if mashing something against its palate, or, in any case, wishing it could.

"Dear God," Nathan said again.

He had not until that moment considered the possibility that the child might be alive.

He left his shotgun in the nest of leaves, because he needed both hands to steady the child's body against his, hold the head firmly to his chest. He and his dog sprinted for the station wagon. Behind him, dawn broke across the lake. Ducks flew unmolested. Forgotten.

At the hospital, two emergency-room doctors sprang into rapid, jerky motion when they saw what Nathan held. They set the infant on a cart, a speck in the middle of an ocean, and unwrapped the sweater. A boy, Nathan saw. A boy still wearing his umbilical cord, a badge of innocence.

As they ran, rolling the cart alongside, one of the doctors pulled off the knit cap. It fell to the linoleum floor unnoticed.

Nathan picked it up, put it in a zippered pocket of his hunting vest. It was so small, that cap; it wouldn't cover Nathan's palm. He moved as close to the door of the examining room as he felt would be allowed.

He heard one of the doctors say, "Throw him out in the woods on an October night, then give him a nice warm sweater and a little hat to hold in his body heat. Now that's ambivalence."

Nathan walked down the hall and bought a cup of hot coffee from a vending machine. It was indeed hot, but that's all that could be said for it.

Twenty or thirty minutes later a doctor came out of that room.

"Doctor," Nathan called, and ran down the hall. The doctor's face looked blank, as if he could not recall where he'd seen Nathan before. "I'm the man who found that baby in the woods."

"Ah, yes," the doctor said. "So you are. Can you stay a few minutes? The police will want to speak with you. If you have to go, please leave your phone number at the desk. I'm sure you understand. They'll want all the details they can get. Try to find who did this thing."

"How is the boy?"

"What kind of shape is he in? Bad shape. Will he survive? Probably. I don't promise, but he's a fighter. Sometimes they're stronger than you can imagine at that age."

"I want to adopt that boy," Nathan said.

"If he survives, you mean."

"Yes. If he survives."

"I'm sorry," the doctor said. "That would not be my department."

He told the story in earnest detail to the police, careful to stress that the real hero was sitting out in the back seat of his station wagon.

"Baby'd be dead if it wasn't for you."

"And Sadie," Nathan said.

"Right. Look. We know you've got stuff to do, but we need you to show us the exact crime scene."

"No inconvenience," Nathan said. "I was on my way back there now, to get my shotgun."

They began walking toward the hospital parking lot together.

"I want to adopt that boy," Nathan said.

"We couldn't tell you nothing about that," the cop

replied.

"I want to adopt that boy," Nathan said to his wife, Flora, over a late brunch. They sat at the kitchen table, Nathan smearing jam on his English muffin. He preferred butter, but was having to watch his waist.

"Don't be absurd," Flora said. She sat with a cigarette high in the crook of her first two fingers, reading the paper. She had the gravelly voice of a drinking woman, which she was not.

Nathan sipped his coffee; it was hot and strong. He felt a pang of loss remembering there would be no roast duck for supper.

"Why is it absurd?"

"Neither one of us is very fond of kids. And we're hardly kids ourselves."

"I like children well enough. I just never thought we'd be all that well suited."

Flora looked up from her paper for the first time. "Just answered your own question, haven't you?"

"This is different. This was meant to be."

She took a puff of her cigarette, set it down on the ashtray, and regarded him briefly. "Nathan," she began. Nathan thought he heard a note of derision. Condescension, even. "I've known you twenty-four years, and you have never before said that anything was 'meant to be.'"

"Maybe in twenty-four years nothing else came into that category."

Flora shook her head. "Anyway, the kid probably has somebody. A mother. They could find the mother."

"If they find her," Nathan said evenly, "they will put her in jail."

"And then it could turn out he has some other kin that would take him."

"Maybe," Nathan said. "We'll see. It just seems to me that when an infant is alone in the woods, slowly dying . . . that child has . . . for all intents and purposes . . . no one."

But when Nathan read the paper the next morning, he found he had supposed incorrectly. The boy had a mother, who had been located. She had attempted to cross a state line, but had instead ended up in an emergency room, hemorrhaging. She had been arrested, though not yet arraigned, and a debate raged over what charges should be brought. Reckless endangerment, reckless disregard for human life. Some said attempted murder, conspiracy to commit murder. The question on seemingly everyone's lips: Why the woods? Why not a hospital or an orphanage? But no answer appeared to be forthcoming.

The article also said that the child, if and when he ever recovered enough to leave the hospital, would be given into the custodial care of his grandmother, Mrs. Ertha Bates, mother of the troubled girl, who lived in a small town an hour's drive away.

And then, finally, it noted that the infant had been found in the woods by a man on a duck-hunting outing with his dog.

Nathan folded up the paper, set it to rest on the end table near the couch, and sat a moment, digesting this new information. He thought about lighting a cigarette, though he'd gone to the trouble to quit them several years ago, and didn't fancy going through all that again.

Then he began to wonder how hard it would be to find this Ertha Bates.

He discovered it would not be difficult at all.

The home of Mrs. Ertha Bates was kept tidy, but it was old. The porch boards creaked and sagged under Nathan's weight.

He rapped on the front door, into which was set an arrangement of teardrop-shaped glass panes forming a half circle.

A curtain slid aside, and a woman's face appeared.

Then the door opened.

She stood on the sill, did not invite him in. She was a woman perhaps his own age, mid-forties—but old-looking, as though used too roughly—with graying hair, a faded-but-clean dress, and a plain white apron.

"Yes?" she said.

Nathan held his hat in front of him. "I'm the man who found the baby in the woods."

"I see."

"Is that all you have to say to me? 'I see'?"

"I can't know what to say to you," she said, "until I know what you've come to say to me."

While they talked, her hands worked across that apron, smoothed and smoothed, as if trying to smooth away . . . what? Nathan wondered.

"I wanted to adopt that boy."

"So I heard."

"But I didn't come to argue that."

245

"Good," she said. "Because I am his flesh and blood."

"Yes," Nathan said. "That is incontrovertible. Now let me tell you something else that also is. That boy would not exist if I had not been in just that place at just that time. I'm not suggesting there was any special heroism involved, or that anyone else couldn't have done the same thing equally well. Only that it wasn't anyone else; it was me. No one can take that from me, any more than they can deny your claim by blood."

"What do you want from me?" she asked, beginning to sound unnerved.

"Only this, and I think it's reasonable: Sometime in the course of that boy's life, I want him to know me. I want you to bring him to me when he's grown. Or half grown. That's up to you. And I want you to introduce me, and say to him, 'This is the man who found you in the woods.' That way he'll know me. I will exist for him."

Ertha Bates stood silent a moment, smoothing. Then she said, "How would I find you?"

Nathan reached into his coat pocket and produced his business card, which advertised his combined bookkeeping and tax-consultation services.

Mrs. Bates accepted the card without looking at it. It disappeared into one big apron pocket. Her eyes found his directly.

"All right, then," she said. "All right. As you say. When I think he's old enough to understand such a thing, I'll bring him around to see you."

"Thank you." Nathan replaced his hat, turned, and took a few creaky steps. Then he looked over his shoulder, hoping she had not gone back inside. She had not. "Does he have a name?" he asked. "Have you picked out a name for him?"

She drew his card out of her apron pocket and peered at it closely, as though her eyes were not good. "Nathan," she said. "He has a name now, then."

"Thank you." Though he knew it was an overly polite gesture, he tipped his hat to her before heading away.

"Thank *you*, sir," she said as he walked off her porch, walked out of the lives of both Ertha and the boy for very nearly fifteen years.

September 23, 1969

Nathan McCann answered the knock at his door to find an older woman standing on his stoop, accompanied by a sullen teenage boy. Hair hung into the boy's eyes; he looked away from Nathan, as if he could establish the matter of his disdain just that simply. Nathan did not enjoy unannounced visits, nor did he initially connect with a memory of having seen these people before.

"Nathan McCann?" the woman asked.

"Yes."

"Nathan McCann, this is Nathan Bates. The boy you found in the woods. I remember at the time you were keen to have this boy for your own. So, tell me, Mr. McCann, do you still feel that same way now? Because I am at my wits' end. This situation is completely outside my ability to cope. I raised five children on what I thought to be normal discipline, but if there's something this boy responds to, I haven't stumbled across it yet. You still want this boy, Mr. McCann? You'd be doing me a great favor. I figure he'd be better off here than as a ward of the state, and that's his next stop, believe me."

"Yes," Nathan said. "I still feel that same way now."

The boy's eyes came up briefly when he said this, then flicked away again.

"Good. I have his things out in the car."

"We'll help you carry them in," Nathan said. "Won't we, Nathan?"

On the trips into the house with the boy's belongings, Nathan felt a pang of regret that Flora had not lived to see the day. She'd teased him unmercifully for feeling it was meant to be.

"You can sleep in my wife's old room," he said to the boy. "What do you go by?"

"What?"

"What do they call you?"

"Oh. Nat."

"Good," Nathan said. "That will avoid some confusion. Gradually we'll take my late wife's things out to the garage. You can make this room entirely yours."

Nat stood with his shoulder on the doorjamb. "You two didn't even sleep together?"

Nathan dropped a suitcase and stood upright, his back poker-straight. He regarded the boy for a moment; the boy met his gaze unswervingly. Nathan felt the weight of these early tests.

"It's not something I'd expect you to understand," he said. "But we loved each other in our way. Maybe it wasn't always the best way, but it was what we could manage."

Then he went around to the back door and let his dog Maggie come into the house. It was a luxury he'd allowed himself, and Maggie, often since Flora's death.

They walked together to Nat's new room.

Nat looked up, seeming stunned. "Is that the dog?"

"No, it's not," Nathan said, sorry to break the bad news, and also sorry it was not. "No, Sadie is long gone. This is Maggie."

"Oh, ok," Nat said, and brushed the stunned look away.

At bedtime, Nathan rapped lightly before letting himself into the boy's room.

"What?" Nat said as Nathan pulled a chair to his bedside.

"I just came in to say good night."

"Oh."

Nathan took the photograph out of the pocket of his sweater and laid it on the edge of the boy's bed.

"That was her," he said. "She was a curly-coated retriever. She was a remarkable dog. I miss her terribly."

Nat picked up the photo, studied it briefly. "Aren't you even going to ask me what I did to get thrown out of the house?"

"No. I thought it best to start fresh with each other. You'll have a birthday coming up next week. We'll celebrate."

"How do you know my birthday?"

"How can I not know your birthday? I found you in the woods on October first, 1954. How could I forget a date like that? You were born the day before, September thirtieth. You'll be fifteen."

"How am I supposed to live here? I don't even know you." It seemed out of context with what Nathan had just told him. "I don't even know this place. This is all completely strange to me. How am I supposed to live here?"

Nathan sighed. "A few minutes at a time, I suppose, at first. I won't pretend it's not a problem for you."

"And you?" the boy asked, even more agitated. "This is not a problem for you?"

"No," Nathan said. "I'm happy to have you here with me."

He turned out the light on his way out of the room.

"I can't believe you're willing to give me a gun," the boy said. "You certainly don't know me very well. I don't want to go duck hunting. It's four o'clock in the goddamn morning. I want to go back to sleep."

"There will be no swearing in this house," Nathan said. "I'm only asking that you try it with me this one time. It you don't like it, I won't ask you to go again."

The boy was sulky and quiet on the drive to the lake, but he reached back to scratch Maggie's head.

"Check to see that the safety is on," Nathan said as they unloaded the car. "And then carry the weapon so it points at nothing. Up across your shoulder, or in the crook of your arm pointing forward and toward the ground."

"But the safety is on."

"With guns it's best to be double safe."

They began the hike to the lake, side by side, Maggie bounding ahead.

"I wish you wouldn't make me ask," the boy said after a short walk. "I wish you would just tell me, and not put me through having to ask."

"When we get there," Nathan said, "I'll show you the place."

About an eighth of a mile later, Nathan said, "Right over there. Under that tree."

The boy walked over and stood looking down at a fresh blanket of the new season's leaves in the near dark. Nathan and Maggie waited until he was done.

The lesson in hunting did not go well. In fact, in time it broke down completely, with Nat leaping up in the air and waving his arms to purposely scare the ducks away.

"Fly away!" he shouted. "Fly away, you idiots, or you're going to get shot!"

They did fly away, the reflection of their collective wings beating across the water.

Then he sat down behind the duck blind and waited to see what Nathan would do.

"The acting out you've been used to doing," Nathan said, "will not be acceptable with me. While you're with me you will behave like a civilized person."

"Great. You want me to shoot things. Very civilized."

"Do you eat fowl?" Nathan asked.

"Do I eat what?"

"Are you a vegetarian?"

"No. I'm not."

"Then, yes, it's civilized. What a man eats, he should be willing to kill. It's not absolutely necessary that he do, but he should at least be willing to. To eat a chicken only if it comes from the market is the height of cowardice and denial. Someone still had to kill it."

Nat rose and walked a few feet away. Kicked at the grass for a moment.

When Nathan looked up again, he found himself staring into the barrel of the boy's gun.

The gun was, of course, filled with light birdshot. And the boy was an inexperienced shooter, but it's hard to miss a substantial target with a shotgun. Plus the kick would raise the shot some, and a pellet through the eye could certainly prove fatal. So it was conceivable, though unlikely, that Nathan could be killed. He weighed and juggled these factors as the boy spoke his piece.

"You can't civilize me," Nat said. "You can't make me stop swearing. Or learn to hunt. Or act like a gentleman, or be 'double safe.' I'll shoot you down before I let you make me into something I'm not."

"I want you to be what you are," Nathan said, "only civilized. And the only way you can stop me is to shoot me dead, so it you're set on stopping me, you'd best go ahead with that now."

The boy's hands trembled on the shotgun for another moment before he let the muzzle drift slightly downward.

Nathan said, "All you've probably needed all this

time was someone who cared enough to insist you behave." And perhaps willing to die to make that happen, he thought.

The boy dropped the shotgun and ran away.

When Nathan arrived back at the station wagon about two hours later, the boy was waiting for him inside. It pleased Nathan to see this, but he didn't make a fuss. He placed his four ducks up front, in canvas sacks: two on the bench seat between them, two on the passenger floor near Nat's feet.

"I won't insist on this," Nathan said, "but it's a lot of work to clean and dress four ducks. I'd appreciate it if you'd help me."

"Why did she do it?" Nat asked.

"I don't know," Nathan said. "I can't imagine."

"Think how it makes me feel."

"I have. Many times."

"Then my grandmother abandons me."

"Cry for yourself for the first of those two events," Nathan said. "You have that due you. But look hard at yourself about the second one. You did something to cause your grandmother to wash her hands of you. I just don't care to know what it was."

"What do I have to do to make you wash your hands of me?"

"There's nothing you could do. I will never wash my hands of you."

They rode the rest of the way home in silence.

Nat joined Nathan in the garage for the cleaning and dressing. The boy wasn't willing to gut, but seemed able to pluck out the feathers.

Nathan said, "We'll put three in the freezer, and I'll roast one for our supper tonight. Have you ever had roast duck?"

"I don't think so."

"You're in for a treat."

They worked in silence a few minutes; then Nathan asked, "What ever happened to your mother, after they let her out of prison?"

"I have no idea," Nat said.

"You never saw her?"

"She never even sent a birthday card."

"I did, though," Nathan said. "I hope they were always passed on to you."

"Yeah, every birthday and every Christmas my grandmother would give me a card and a present. And she would say, 'Here. This is from the man who found you in the woods.'"

His voice sounded different, which caused Nathan to look up, but the boy was looking down at his work, expressionless.

"Then why did you act surprised that I know your birthday?"

The boy only shrugged.

"They may not have been the best, most appropriate gifts," Nathan said. "I don't know that I ever gave you what you wanted. Because I didn't have the advantage of knowing you. Knowing your likes and dislikes."

"I don't think that's the important thing, though," Nat said. "I think the thing is, you never once forgot."

They sat down together to a roast-duck supper with applesauce and mashed potatoes.

"This is good," the boy said.

Nathan thought perhaps they had turned a corner. He expected that things might turn out all right between them after all.

The following day the boy was arrested for trying to rob a gas station with the shotgun Nathan had barely taught him to use. He'd taken a hacksaw from the garage and cut through the lock to gain access to the gun rack.

Nathan drove to the jail, where he was allowed to see the boy.

"Good," Nat said. "You've come to post my bail."

"No," Nathan said. "I'll come see you every visiting day. But I won't put up bond for you. Because I know you'll run away. You're going to stay in here until your hearing, and then you'll go into the juvenile-detention system and pay for what you did."

The boy said nothing for a long time. Then he said, "You're right about one thing. I would have run out on the bail."

"Why did you do this?" Nathan asked.

The boy shrugged. "Everyone else does bad things. Why shouldn't I?"

"I don't. Lots of people don't."

The boy sighed and brushed the hair back out of his eyes. "I believed you," he said. "I believed that as long as you were alive you'd never wash your hands of me. Never stop trying to civilize me. I was trying to get far away."

"I see."

"Wash your hands of me now?"

"No," Nathan said.

Two days later, on the boy's birthday, Nathan came to visit. He brought a birthday cupcake—a whole cake seemed excessive under the circumstances—half a roast duck in foil in a paper grocery sack, and a small wrapped gift.

"Open it now?" the boy asked.

The guard looked over their shoulders to assure himself the present was no more than Nathan had claimed. They'd allowed him to enter with a wrapped gift because it was small, light, and soft, with no real potential to be dangerous.

The boy tore off the paper and stared at the gift.

"It looks like a little tiny cap," he said, turning it over in his fingers.

"It is."

The guard backed off to the corner of the room again.

"Who could wear a cap this small?"

"You, when you were only one day old."

"You've kept it all this time? Why give it to me now?"

"I wanted you to know that she at least had some ambivalence. She left you to die, but part of her wanted you to live. She was trying to keep you warm."

"That's not a lot of consolation," the boy said.

"No, but it's some. We don't always get much. I'm sorry if it's not a good gift. I still don't really know you. I don't know what kind of things you like."

"No, it's good," the boy said. "It's a good present." He sat quietly for a minute, then said, "The baseball mitt was good, too. I really liked that."

"Good," Nathan said. "That's two. That's something."

Nearly a year into the boy's sentence at juvenile detention, Nathan had a conversation with a guard on his way out the door. This was a guard he'd come to know slightly. Roger was his name.

"Three times a week like clockwork," Roger said. "I could set my watch by you."

"Does that seem remarkable?" Nathan asked.

"It does. When you consider he knew you four days before he got himself in custody."

"No," Nathan said. "I've known him all his life."

Roger lifted his eyebrows slightly. "He's lying, then?"

"Not lying. He sees it differently than I do. But I'm not his father."

"Why, then? Why the remarkable commitment?"

Nathan had heard once of an Eastern religion whose devotees believed if you saved someone's life, you were forever responsible for his soul. Or was that the American Indian? No matter. Nathan didn't believe a word of it, anyway.

"Why not?" he asked. "What else have I done with my life that's remarkable?"

WITNESS TO BREATH

Every night on her way home she goes by Phan's Round-the-Clock Market. Usually about three. Different reasons; different things. On a good night maybe cigarettes.

Maybe gum. Bad night maybe aspirin. Pepto Bismol.

Tonight she should stock up on Tampax. Which is good news, really. A few days off coming up. But she can't go into Phan's and get them because something has gone down.

She could walk by, walk away. But she stands with the crowd, looking, to see what went down. Better than sitting home in the dark, in that little apartment. Listening to sirens. Wondering. Watching strobe red reflect on beige walls, right through the curtains. You're no safer behind those locked doors. No safer at all. That's just a joke you tell yourself when something goes down.

Crime scene tape, all around. Yellow, with that special way of flipping in the breeze. Twisting. And cop cars. People crane their necks to see. All her neighbors, most likely, but there's nobody here she knows. Maybe there's nobody anywhere she knows. She used to know people, but she's not sure if that counts. It's like a driver's license, knowing somebody. It doesn't last forever all on its own.

Phan's wife, crying. Really hysterical crying.

An old man wasted on the floor. You can see him through the open door into the market. This bulky abandoned thing, like one of those whales that swim up on the beach. That's what she thinks he's like. Because he just looks like that, and because nobody really knows why that happens, either.

Around the head of the old man, a pool of blood. Not all that big. Half a pint, maybe. Shiny. Black in the fluorescent lights of Phan's Round-the-Clock Market.

She goes in there every night. It could have been her in there tonight. But it wasn't. So she goes home.

At home, she triple-locks the door. Steps out of the short leather skirt, the devil heels. All the time listening to that noise, that weird noise. Like a person crying out loud. No, weirder. And louder. Goes into the bathroom, washes off her makeup. Slips off the rest of her clothes, dropping them on the floor. Lies down and tries to sleep. But that noise.

So she gets up again. Puts on jeans, flats. A fake fur over nothing. And goes back downstairs to the super's apartment and pounds on his door.

"It can wait 'til morning," he yells through the door.

"Hell it can," she says, and pounds harder.

The door swings open. "What?" Irv in a brown corduroy robe, black hair tumbled, face unshaven, red-eyed. Like she woke him up.

"How in god's name can you sleep through that noise?"

The look on his face develops into something. He leans out into the hall, closer to her, like step one in a conspiracy. "Tragic, ain't it?"

"Damn right it's tragic. I need some sleep."

"No, I mean the dog."

"That's a dog?"

"You know whose dog, right?"

"I didn't even know it was a dog."

"Guy got popped down at Phan's. That's whose dog that is. He's mourning."

She waits before responding, to let the details drop in. Thought number one to spring up out of that eddy: That old man lived right in this building. Thought two: How can the dog be mourning? Who told him what happened?

"So he just howls until his voice is too weak from hunger? That's not very humane."

"I called the Animal Regulation Department. They'll come pick him up. But not 'til morning. You wanta hear something weird? Dog started howling the minute it happened. I looked at my watch. The Dating Game was just starting. Ten minutes later Mrs. Greavy from 3G knocks on my door, says it happened ten minutes ago. No reason, either. Mrs. Phan gave the kid all her money. He was on his way out. Old man's just standing there. Just standing there. And on the way out the kid pops him. Shoots the old man in the head. No reason. I tell you, this world has gone crazy. And that same minute his dog starts to howl. Fucking weird if you ask me. Did you know a dog's hearing is ten times better than our own? So he heard the shot alright. But what I want to know is, how did he know who got it? I mean, that makes you think. That makes you wonder what else that dog has that's ten times better than our own. You know?"

"Fascinating, Irv. Any idea how I might get some sleep?"

"Unless maybe you want to take him out. Maybe he needs to go out. Maybe the old guy left some dog food lying around. Maybe feed him and take him out; he might feel better. Might sleep some. I could let you in with my pass key."

She scans the hall ceiling. Sighs. Shuffles impatience. Says, "At this point I'll try anything."

Irv swings the old man's apartment door wide. "Lock up before you go."

The old man's light is on. Like he knew he'd be back in just a minute, and it seems sad to her, how he could be so stunningly wrong. The walls are all covered with posters of movies that stopped playing generations before she was born. All starring Myrna Loy, whoever that is. Was.

And the dog.

Just sitting on the floor, looking at them. She's seen this dog before. Three times a day, like clockwork, the old guy took him out. Weird-looking dog. Tan-coated. All tall and skinny, like a wolfhound, only not a wolfhound for real, just all tall and skinny like one. His legs are so long and skinny they look like one might snap off if you weren't careful. The old guy must've been careful. And a long narrow muzzle all white with age, and these big brown eyes. So he's just sitting there, looking like the oldest dog in the world. Looking too old and fragile to be alive. Just looking at her.

Then he tips back his head and lets out another dose of that sound. It makes her think of a really smooth, skillful jazz saxophonist, the kind that can hit one note and make you cry. Now he looks at her again. Sitting with his front paws just ever so lightly on the carpet, like the ground hurts wherever he touches it.

And she's not answering Irv, just looking back at the dog, so Irv says, "Lock up I said, okay? Not that there's nothing to steal in here, but still."

"Wait. Don't go away. What am I supposed to do with him?"

"I dunno. Feed him? Take him out? This was all your idea. Maybe there's food in the kitchen."

Irv goes in there to see. The dog doesn't even follow him with his eyes. Just looks at her, then lies down slowly. Kind of dainty almost. Reaches out with those long matchstick legs one baby step at a time until he's lying down, then crosses them one over the other.

Irv comes back. "Here's one can of dog food. All the old guy had. End of the month, you know? He gets his S.S.I. checks on the first. Lock up when you're all done in here."

"Wait. Did he have any family?"

"Nah. Pretty much alone in the world."

"So, who's going to go get the dog out of the pound?"

"I dunno. Maybe he could get adopted."

"Nobody would adopt that dog. He's weird-looking. And he's too old."

The dog turns his head away. Turns it to one side, and sets his chin down, barely touching one matchstick leg.

"Yeah, he's that alright. Oldest dog I ever seen. Probably as old as the old guy."

"You think a dog is seventy or eighty?"

"Well, maybe in dog years."

"Go back to sleep, Irv. I'll lock up."

When Irv is down the hall and gone, and there's no one to hear her and think she's a fool, she addresses the dog directly. "Sorry for what I said." The dog raises his head and looks at her again. Steady, calm. Unflinching. Guileless. "But it's the truth, anyway. I'm not gonna lie to you. I'm not gonna say he's coming back, or somebody'll give you a nice home. Why lie to a dog?" Then she thinks, Why talk to a dog at all? But it seemed like a right thing at the time. "You want to go out?"

The dog stands up on those stilts like he never once did before. There's a leash hanging on the door, so she clips it on him. And they walk down the stairs. Down to the street. Out into the cold city pre-morning dark.

Dog just stands there, looking down toward Phan's Round-the-Clock Market. She thinks he wants to go down there but he's too polite to pull on the leash. So they just stand. A few minutes later he looks up at her with those big eyes.

The can of Alpo feels heavy in her coat pocket.

She breathes steam. Dog breathes steam. The street

breathes steam, from the manhole covers. They all stand there and breathe together—young woman, old dog, cold city—just alive at the same moment like that. Then Dog lifts his leg against nothing, way out at a right angle. He's so tall, it's almost at the level of her waist. He spatters the sidewalk, which also breathes steam. Then, when he's done peeing, he turns to go back in.

He wants to go back to his own apartment, but she wants him to come to hers and he's too polite to argue.

In the night she wakes up knowing someone is in the room with her. She opens her eyes. But it's only Dog, sitting next to her bed, one fragile paw raised, as if to touch her, but not quite.

"What, Dog?" she says. "I know you want something."

Dog picks up the paw again. Touches the bedcovers, reaching a little further this time.

"Can't you be a little more specific? Are you trying to tell me you want up on the bed? Did that old guy let you up on the bed? Shit. Just my luck. Okay, whatever."

She slides back a little, and Dog comes up. Not jumps, just steps up, one long leg at a time. Four giant steps. Then he circles five times before lying down. Curls up with his head near hers, near the top of the bed. Just in that moment before sleep, his warm, regular breath across her cheek.

In the morning Irv knocks. She leaves the dog sleeping

on the bed and goes to see.

"Animal Regulation is here," he says. "What the hell happened to the dog?"

"No idea. Maybe family came and took him."

"Guy didn't have no family."

"Friend, then."

"Did you do something cruel? Ditch that poor old dog out in the cold by himself?"

She opens the door wide, so Irv can look right into the bedroom. Looks over her own shoulder, to make sure he can see. Dog looks back over his shoulder at them. With some kind of knowing, but what kind she's not sure.

"Nobody was gonna take that dog out of the pound, Irv, you know that."

"Right. I guess a friend must've come by to get him, then."

"Only friend he's got now. He have a name, that dog?"

"Hell if I know."

She closes the door and goes back to bed beside Dog.

When she wakes up at four p.m., she opens the can of Alpo and calls Dog to come get it. Dog does not. She puts it on a plate, and serves it to Dog in bed. He reaches his skinny white muzzle out to barely touch it, slow and soft, like he did to her face in the night. Then he sets his chin down.

"Okay, you're just upset," she says. "I gotta get ready for work." Not that it takes her six hours to get ready, but the inside part, she just needs more and more time for that these days. "Don't worry, I'll take you out before I go."

She looks over her shoulder at Dog, whose eyes seem to say, Better not to go at all. Or was that a voice in her own head? It's hard sometimes, to know if it's a dog or your own head, telling you things. They study each other's face.

"Look, don't judge me," she says, and he sets his chin down again.

She's pretty sure she called that one wrong. That was her own head.

She sweeps into the bathroom. Thinks about Tampax. Realizes she really won't be working tonight. It breathes out of her, all that preparation, leaving her pounds lighter and able to smile. She sticks her head into the bedroom and smiles at Dog. Who else?

"Never mind. I'll stay here with you. But we have to walk down to Phan's." Then she thinks, No. He doesn't want to. Then she knows, Yeah. He does.

Dog walks slowly everywhere, but she thinks he walks even slower down to Phan's. Now and then reaching his long neck down to almost touch his nose to the snow-dusted sidewalk. When they reach the market door, he stops. First she thinks, He knows something. Then she thinks, He knows he's not allowed in.

She leads him in.

Over to the spot on the floor where the old man's blood pooled, but it's clean now. Perfect white linoleum. She thinks maybe it never happened. Maybe she saw it in a dream. She thinks she might have had a dream last night about black blood on a white linoleum beach.

Mrs. Phan runs around the counter, agitated, tiny, spewing. "No dog, not allowed, you go out with him, I got health codes."

"I just want him to see," she says.

"See what? Nothing here for dog to see."

"It was his dog, though. The old man's. I just want him to understand, you know?"

She looks down at Dog, who looks back. Those big dark eyes. It seems he does understand, certainly better than Mrs. Phan, maybe better than she herself.

"Nothing for dog to see. You take him outside now. I got health codes."

"He can smell, you know? How the trail sort of ends here."

"All disinfected. Nothing to smell. All clean now. Go."

"I need Tampax. And dog food."

Mrs. Phan races around behind an aisle, grabs a box of Tampax, scoops three big cans of Alpo into her arms. Dumps the whole load over to her, helping her balance everything, then turns her and pushes her from behind. Pushes her to the door. "On the house. No charge. Now go."

She tucks Alpo into her big coat pockets as they walk home together.

Together. That seems like a funny word. She thinks that, to Mrs. Phan, customers are known quantities. Mrs. Phan knew what kind of Tampax, what brand of dog food. An odd comfort, to be known, even by Mrs. Phan.

"She seemed afraid of more than just her health codes," she tells Dog out loud.

She looks down at Dog, who looks back. This time she tries not to read too much in.

Five days later, the three cans of Alpo still sit on her kitchen counter. She takes the contents of the original one out of the refrigerator, as she does many times every day, nukes it in the microwave to take off the chill, and presents it to Dog, pretending this time he will eat. He does not. She offers him a dish of clean water.

He approaches it with the tip of his long muzzle. Almost touching the still surface, but not quite. As he does to her face every night when she's barely asleep.

It strikes her that his movements are somehow dignified. Not that she never noticed; more that she never applied that exact word. But that's the word, all right. Dignified.

He reaches out his tongue and licks the surface of the water three times. She sits down hard on the bed, knowing things she didn't let herself know before just now. That he'll die if he doesn't eat. That she has to take him to the vet tonight. Which means she has to work.

She looks down at Dog for input, but his eyes are closed.

She tries to go to work. But it doesn't happen right. Oh, she walks down the boulevard. One car slows, but she keeps walking. Says that prayer she says every working night of her life. Don't let this be the night I buy it. Protect me one more time. After tonight I'm out. Not that she thinks God is stupid. But if she believes it every time she says it, isn't that still sincere?

She leans on a mailbox, lights a cigarette. Thinks, If this is the night I buy it, he's stuck in that apartment to die. And that's wrong. Double jeopardy wrong. Nobody should have to go there twice.

She runs two movies in her head. In the first, the guy's a violent wacko and she has to beg for her life. She tells him her dog is sick at home. Asks him if he ever had a dog, waiting. Needing him. And he lets her go. Not so much out of compassion, but because she killed the mood completely talking about his dog.

In the second version he slits her throat while the words are still just a picture in her head.

She crushes out the cigarette and goes home. Carries Dog down to the street. She wants him to be too heavy, but he's not. Bones now. Just bones.

Hails a cab. She has money for the cab but not for the vet.

At the emergency vet hospital, in an examining room, she holds Dog's head, waiting alone with him until the vet comes in. The vet is tall, and older, with a nice face.

"I don't have any money." She was going to have him look after Dog first, then tell him. But while she was waiting she thought, Maybe legally he could hold Dog until I pay. Dog hasn't got that much time. "I'm sort of between careers," she says, which is weak but true. "I'll leave my purse if you want. It has all my I.D. in it. Like collateral. Until I pay. If you want."

The vet steadies both sides of Dog's bony head. Looks into his eyes. "Your dog is very old," he says.

"I *will* pay you. Really."

"Sometimes you don't think, when you get a dog. That he could become a financial liability."

"He's not even my dog. He belonged to this old guy who got killed in a robbery the other day."

"That was nice of you to want to help him."

"Yeah, funny thing about that. It's not the usual me. He hasn't eaten a bite since then. Hardly even drinks water."

The vet sighs. "I can do all kinds of things, if you're sure you want me to. Run expensive blood tests. See if I can find something. But we both know why he won't eat."

"You could force feed him or something."

"I could feed him through an i.v. drip. Prolong his life. But for how long? He's elderly. Maybe he's just ready. Dogs know sometimes when they're ready. I think maybe he just wants to die with dignity. He seems like a dignified dog."

She sits down. She hasn't eaten much either.

First she thinks, I'll go out and work. And he'll put Dog on an i.v. and Dog will come around and we'll do that together thing a little while longer. But it seems wrong. Sell out her own dignity to earn enough money to buy up the last of his.

"So, what do you do, give him a shot or something?"

"It's up to you, but I think that's probably best."

She nods.

Vet fills a hypodermic needle. "You can stay if you want, or wait out front."

"I'll stay." She holds Dog around his frail neck; he feels calm. And she starts to cry. "I don't know why I'm crying. I hardly know this dog." But then she knows why. "Can you imagine that? Having somebody who cares that much if you live or die, that he'd starve himself to death if you didn't come home?"

"Don't act like dogs are such a well-kept secret. Why do you think people have them?"

"I never knew, really. I never had one. Never liked them. Well. Never knew one, I guess."

The vet is ready now, with the shot. She talks to Dog, but not out loud. Because she doesn't know this vet, and it's personal. And he shouldn't hear.

She says, I know you were here. I'll howl tonight, because you're gone. She says, I am your witness.

Vet says, "There's no charge for that."

On her way out she thanks him, and tells him her name is Estelle. Not that she thinks he really cares. But she cares. She thinks somebody should know that her name is Estelle.

She doesn't eat for three days, in Dog's honor.

She gives the unopened dog food back to Mrs. Phan, because that seems like the dignified thing to do.

ACKNOWLEDGMENTS for Subway Dancer and Other Stories

"Blue Dog in the Crazy Truck" first appeared in *Michigan Quarterly Review*

"Bloodlines" first appeared in *Ploughshares* and was cited in *Best American Short Stories 2002* and reprinted in the NYT best-selling anthology Dog is my Co-Pilot (Crown '03)

"Hurricane Laura" first appeared in *The Virginia Quarterly Review*

"The Expatriate" first appeared in *Red Cedar Review*

"Disappearances" first appeared in *Glimmer Train*

"Five Singing Gardeners and One Dead Stranger" first appeared in *Literal Latte* and was nominated for The Pushcart Prize

"Subway Dancer and Snake" first appeared in *The Antioch Review*

"Reasons For Love" first appeared in *Pangolin Papers*

"Dancing With Elinor" first appeared in *The Gettysburg Review*

"Kid Trees" first appeared in *Sidewalks*

"The Last Younger Man" first appeared in *Eureka Literary Magazine*

"Requiem For a Flamer" first appeared in *Quarterly West* and was nominated for The Pushcart Prize

"The Worry Stone" first appeared in *Manoa*

"The Man Who Found You in the Woods" first appeared in *The Sun* and was cited in *Best American Short Stories 2002*

"Witness to Breath" first appeared in *New Letters*

Author's Note:

I have never understood why the words "literary" or "short stories" would hurt a book's chances, but I am delighted to see what appears to be a resurgence of short fiction. Into that resurgence I offer *Subway Dancer and Other Stories*, a collection that has been waiting patiently through the publication of many novels.

Although some of these stories have been added more recently, the core of this collection predates the success of *Pay It Forward* in the year 2000. So of course my agents and I were sure that finding a good home for a collection of well-honored stories would be about as hard as slipping on the ice. And at the same time we were looking to sell reprint rights for my earlier novel *Funerals for Horses*. Which we also figured should be easy.

And yet this is the first publication, in book form, of these stories.

And the *Funerals for Horses* reprint came out in 2012.

This is not to say we couldn't find a home for either.

Just that *Funerals for Horses* was called "more literary" by those who offered to take it on, and, bizarrely, they did not say that like it was a good thing. And *Subway Dancer* was, after all, a short story collection. Same tone.

We agreed that we would decline these offers, instead reserving the books for someone who used the words "literary" and "short stories" more like a compliment.

The first good news: my day has arrived! Short stories are making a comeback, and literary fiction is once again viewed with respect, and sought after by many readers.

The additional good news is that I had time to add some newer stories, publish each and every one in a literary or small circulation magazine of good reputation, get a couple nominated for the Pushcart Prize, have two cited in *Best American Short Stories* in the same year, and see one reprinted in the very successful Bark Magazine anthology *Dog is My Co-Pilot*.

Another odd phenomenon occurred during the waiting: several of these stories rose up and announced their intention to become full-length novels. "The Man Who Found You in the Woods" went on to become my novel *When I Found You*. "The Worry Stone" fleshed out into *Second Hand Heart*. And "Kid Trees", after a number of title changes, became my Young Adult novel *The Year of my Miraculous Reappearance*. So if you're reading along, and something rings familiar, that's probably why.

I went back and forth a bit over whether to include

them. I certainly don't want you to feel you're buying something you already bought once before. But it's only three out of fourteen, and I thought it might be of interest to some readers to see how I can be so sure I have a short piece, only to have it blossom into something much greater.

I also thought the chances were slim that the reader who picks up this book will have read each and every one of those novels. If you are the exception to that rule, thank you for being such a complete and faithful reader of my work, and I hope you approve of my decision to include them.

-Catherine

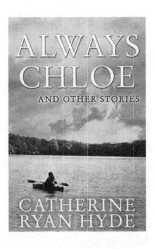

By the bestselling author of *Don't Let Me Go* and *Pay It Forward*, this captivating short story collection features ALWAYS CHLOE, the long-awaited novella sequel to *Becoming Chloe*, Hyde's award-winning novel.

Jordy and Chloe are living above a restaurant in Morro Bay, the first place they landed after their trip down the Big Sur Coast. But Jordy has a boyfriend now, an old flame who's come back into his life in a big way.

Chloe stretches herself as far as she can go to give them her blessing, but her issues about living—or even sleeping—alone turn this happy reunion into a potential disaster. Chloe stops eating, stops sleeping, stops paddling her beloved and battered blue kayak in the bay.

No one knows how to help her. When her friend Old

Ben, the man who runs the fuel dock nearby, gives her some advice, his words could either save the day or send her out to sea forever, depending on her unique mind's understanding of them.

A heart-wrenching stand-alone novella, and an answer to the many readers who asked for a sequel to *Becoming Chloe*, ALWAYS CHLOE is ultimately about the struggle to balance others' needs with our own—and exactly how expansive and forgiving the human heart can be.

This collection also includes four previously published short stories, including "Breakage," which won honors in the Tobias Wolff award, and "The Lion Lottery," which was cited in Best American Short Stories.

BUY YOUR COPY TODAY!

About Catherine Ryan Hyde

Catherine Ryan Hyde is the author of 20 published and forthcoming books. Her newer novels include *When I Found You, Second Hand Heart, Don't Let Me Go,* and *When You Were Older.* New Kindle editions of her earlier titles *Funerals for Horses, Earthquake Weather and Other Stories, Electric God,* and *Walter's Purple Heart* are now available. Her newest ebook title is *The Long Steep Path: Everyday Inspiration from the Author of PAY IT FORWARD,* her first book-length creative nonfiction. Forthcoming frontlist titles are *Walk Me Home* and *Where We Belong.*

She is co-author, with publishing industry blogger Anne R. Allen, of *How to Be a Writer in the E-Age... and Keep Your E-Sanity!*

Her best-known novel, *Pay It Forward,* was adapted into a major motion picture, chosen by the American Library Association for its Best Books for Young Adults list, and translated into more than 23 languages for distribution in over 30 countries. The paperback was released in October 2000 by Pocket Books and quickly became a national bestseller. *Love in the Present Tense* enjoyed bestseller status in the UK, where it broke the top ten, spent five weeks on the national bestseller list, was reviewed on a major TV book club, and shortlisted for a Best Read of the Year award at the British Book Awards. Both *Becoming Chloe* and *Jumpstart the World* were included on the ALA's Rainbow List, and *Jumpstart the World* was a finalist for two Lambda Literary Awards.

More than 50 of her short stories have been published in The Antioch Review, Michigan Quarterly Review, The Virginia Quarterly Review, Ploughshares, Glimmer Train and many other journals, and in the anthologies Santa Barbara Stories and California Shorts and the bestselling anthology Dog is my Co-Pilot. Her stories have been honored in the Raymond Carver Short Story Contest and the Tobias Wolff Award and nominated for Best American Short Stories, the O'Henry Award, and the Pushcart Prize. Three have been cited in Best American Short Stories.

Catherine is founder and former president (2000-2009) of the Pay It Forward Foundation. As a professional public speaker she has addressed the National Conference on Education, twice spoken at Cornell University, met with Americorps members at the White House and shared a dais with Bill Clinton.

For more information, please visit the author at catherineryanhyde.com. You can also learn more about

Catherine by picking up your copy of *The Long Steep Path*!

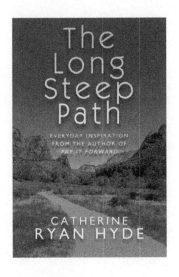

Also by Catherine Ryan Hyde

Diary of a Witness

The Day I Killed James

Chasing Windmills

The Year of My Miraculous Reappearance

Love in the Present Tense

Becoming Chloe

Pay It Forward

<u>Nonfiction</u>

The Long, Steep Path: Everyday Inspiration from the Author of Pay It Forward

How to be a Writer in the E-Age...And Keep Your E-Sanity

Made in the USA
Las Vegas, NV
21 September 2021

30779728R00166